Her Purr-fect Christmas Mate

Copyright © 2022 by Zoe Chant

Cover and internal artwork © 2022 Jess Lang

Cover design © 2022 by Marie Hodgkinson

All rights reserved.

No portion of this book may be reproduced in any form without written permission from the publisher or author, except as permitted by U.S. copyright law.

Her Purr-fect Christmas Mate

Zoe Chant

1

PEONY

The cheerful tones of a Christmas carol jingled from Peony's pocket. She precariously balanced her pile of books in one arm and dug around in her candycane-patterned work apron until she found her phone.

It was the day before Christmas Eve, and she had a good idea who would be calling. One of her regulars—the ones who hadn't made it into the shop to pick up their orders, or the ones who risked fate every year by leaving their present shopping to the last possible minute and begged her to find a miracle copy of the season's top sellers when the shelves had already been picked bare.

Good news, Mr. Asterley, I kept a copy aside for you . . . She was already imagining what she would say, when she saw the name attached to the call.

Mom.

Her stomach clenched as she dismissed the call.

I already know what she's going to say. And I'm at work! I'm too busy to talk now. She'll understand. Excuses flew through her mind faster and thicker than the snowflakes whirling around outside the bookstore windows. None of them helped with the guilt.

Her family couldn't wait to see her for Christmas Eve dinner. And she couldn't wait for Christmas to be over.

I used to love Christmas. What happened? Silly question. She knew what had happened. Christmas had been fun when she was a kid, but now, every year it was *You haven't found your mate yet?* And *Poor Peony, almost thirty and still no idea what her inner animal is.* The fact that they said it with love only made it worse.

Everyone in Peony's huge and hectic family was a shifter, but, unlike other magical families, their inner animals stayed locked away until they met their mate. On top of that, shifter forms weren't inherited in her family. Her inner animal could be anything: a griffin like her older brother . . . a pegasus like her mom . . . a flying silver snake like her uncle . . .

Or a unicorn, like her little sister. Not that that was the reason she was dreading Christmas extra this year. The knowledge that her little sister would be there with her mate and her baby bump and her magically wonderful shifter form, and she would still be plain old Peony.

At least I'll have SOME good news to share this Christmas. She juggled her phone back into her apron pocket and rubbed the shiny *Manager* badge above her nametag. Mr. Blanderley had called her into his office a few days before, and honestly, she'd half expected that it was all over and he was going to fire her. Instead, he'd given her the promotion she'd been dreaming of since she started working at the bookstore.

So why does it feel so hollow?

Because it's just a job. Because my real life hasn't started yet. How can it, when I don't know what my inner animal is?

What if I'm a water horse and books don't fit in my new, damp lifestyle? Or a griffin who thinks books are nothing more than some padding to line my nest?

Her heart sank.

Why bother trying to achieve anything if it might all be swept away when I find out who I really am?

She swallowed. Oh, right. *That* was why she maybe felt the teensiest, tiniest, ittiest bittiest bit not her usual happy perky self.

She paused in the middle of checking her pile of books against orders in the system, and her reflection stared back at her from the computer screen. Her dark curls were pinned back behind a pair of reindeer antlers festooned with holly. Her berry-red lipstick glowed against her brown skin.

But had the shadows under her eyes been that deep when she'd started work? And where was her smile? Sure, the shop was closed for the day and there weren't any customers around, but as soon as she was done with these orders, she had a party to prep for.

Parties were fun. Where was her fun face?

The Hypatia Bookstore took up the old main foyer of the Hypatia Building, a grand Beaux-Arts building that groaned with history and old-world elegance. At least, a better-maintained version of it might have done. In reality, the Hypatia mostly just groaned. Pre-war plumbing fought it out with pre-war wiring for which of them would break next, and if the ancient chandelier that loomed beneath the foyer's vaulted stained-glass ceiling was ever lit again, it would probably send the whole place up in flames.

The bookstore was the only business left in what had once been a sophisticated arcade on the ground floor, patronized by the wealthy and no doubt incredibly stylish and good-looking people who lived in the magnificent apartments above. These days, Peony was the only long-term resident alongside a revolving door of students and tourists misled about the current less-than-sophisticated status of the apartments.

But Peony loved it. She loved the mystery. The grandeur. The *potential*. The Hypatia had so much history—and it could have so much future, too.

If she won the lottery . . .

Hah. I'd have to play the lottery first. And that means I'd need to be able to afford a lottery ticket. Peony ignored the little voice in her head that said, *You'd need to be a type of animal that cares about old architecture, too.*

Peony might not have a mate. She didn't know what her inner animal was. But she could throw a mean end-of-year party for her beloved bookshop and its employees, and that had to count for something, right?

For one night, the Hypatia Bookstore shone. Who cared about worn-out utilities and glitchy internet when glowing fairy lights turned *faded* into *mysterious*? Who worried about that one soft patch of flooring when she walled it off with bookshelves so nobody could accidentally sink into it? And who would even notice the rest of the Hypatia Building looming dark and ominously damp behind the fairytale bookshop in its foyer when these three hundred square feet of it were bursting with light and music and fun?

Not Peony, that was who.

The party was a raging success. Peony had finagled the measly budget Mr. Blanderley gave her to manage gifts for staff and their families, delicious canapés from the deli across the street, and fizzy wine and mocktails.

"Oh yes," she heard Mr. Blanderley say from across the room as she made her way to the mic. "It's all the new manager's doing. Really, I'm astonished it took this long . . ."

Her heart glowed as she hopped up onto the makeshift stage and looked out across the room. She knew every shelving unit by heart. After the weeks leading up to Christmas, she could even label the gaps in the rows of books lining them. The quiet teenager who'd come in every Saturday for a month and stared at the graphic novels without touching them before finally buying the first volume of *Heartstopper*; the older woman she would swear was his mother or aunt who'd swept in the next day and picked up the rest of the set; the genteel-looking gentleman who'd hunted for the most bloodthirsty pirate adventure novels he could find; the whole empty shelf where a harried dad had bought multiple full sets of that popular kids' series with the unicorns because his daughters would raise hell if one of them got to read any of the books before the others.

But the books were only half the story. The people who were celebrating tonight were her family-away-from-home. *My family-away-from-mateless-guilt*, she thought, guiltily. Adrian had worked here for years—he could find a special order for a customer even if the book had been out of print for decades. Muriel knew everything there was to know about TikTok trends. Then there were the part-timers, like Jamal, who only needed to look at a customer and he knew the perfect book for them.

He needed more hours, too. Peony made a mental note to look at the roster first thing after the holiday.

Not all the party-goers were employees of the bookstore. Other people from the building were always welcome at the Hypatia's end-of-year party, and some customers had either managed to sneak in after closing or had lingered around the shelves when they heard it was party night. Mr. Blanderley was here as well, and the usual crowd of half-familiar faces: *Investors*, Peony thought vaguely, and other local business-owners.

"Thank you all so much for coming out this evening," she began, her voice ringing clearly over the crowd. Mingled cheers and whoops answered her, and her cheeks pinked. "It's been another wonderful year at the Hypatia. Sales numbers are . . ." She flicked over a page on the clipboard by the mic and laughed as her colleagues groaned and pretended to run away. "Not important! It's Christmas, and we're here to celebrate! Maybe even longer than you RSVP'd for, if the snow keeps up."

More laughter. She made more, even worse, jokes, thanking everyone who'd come to support the store, until Mr. Blanderley started to look impatient.

Okay, time to wrap it up. She couldn't keep the smile off her face as she swept her eyes across the crowd one last time. Why had she been so down, earlier? Even if her magical life was lacking, she was so happy here.

My real life can't be any better than this, whatever it turns out to be.

"Once again, thank you all for your support of Hypatia Bookstore this year. I can promise you that next year will be even more exciting. We've got an incredible line-up of events planned, with all your favorite storytellers—"

Cheers.

"—murder mysteries—"

More cheers. Was it possible to die from smiling too much?

"—and who knows, maybe we'll even fix the leak in the ocean sciences section!"

Laughter and more cheers. Except from Mr. Blanderley. She probably shouldn't have made a joke at the expense of the maintenance he was meant to be in charge of, but that last sip of bubbly wine had gone to her head and . . .

Peony's voice faded away. The room went muffled.

Standing next to Mr. Blanderley was the sexiest man she'd ever laid eyes on.

Holy heck, she thought, light-headed. *I didn't know they made them like that outside of romance novel covers.*

He was tall, dark, and *delicious*. Hair like jet, pale skin, illegally sharp cheekbones, and eyes that caught her and pinned her like a butterfly beneath a cat's claws.

Some people were good-looking. Some people were handsome. This man was *hot*. He exuded sexiness. She couldn't look at him without thinking of sex. And she couldn't look away from him.

Who is he? She didn't recognize him from the guest list. Was he someone's partner? A nasty feeling twisted inside her. Jealousy. She'd only seen the guy for ten seconds and she was instantly, seethingly jealous of whoever got to take him home at the end of the night.

She fumbled the end of her speech and handed off the mic to Mr. Blanderley. He cleared his throat directly into the microphone, and she barely even winced, because all her focus was still on Mr. Illegal Cheekbones. Her boss blended into the echoey nothing the rest of the universe had blurred into.

The guy was looking at her. He was *looking at her*. His eyes were bright and sharp as broken glass, and he was *looking at her*, and maybe she should take a left here into the Mysteries section because she needed to find out a way to murder whoever this guy had come in with and steal him for herself.

". . . under the management of Mrs. Fisher, this year's party will be the last party . . ."

Parts of Mr. Blanderley's speech made it to her ears, but her brain wasn't listening. The man was still looking at her. His eyebrows drew together and his lips—oh god, his *lips*—puckered slightly. Was it a scowl? A frown? Was he frowning at *her*?

Was she . . . was she staring at him like a complete lunatic?

Mr. Blanderley's voice took on a distinctly sour tone. ". . . pleased to announce the sale of the Hypatia to Mr. Mordecai Leith, who has proposed the redevelopment of the site for an exciting new multi-purpose complex . . ."

Peony's brain finally caught up with reality. She watched the man—Mordecai Leith—stalk up to the stage, and horror crashed through her.

"Good evening." His voice was too good to be true. And it was awful, too. As awful as the unpleasant glint in his eyes as he said he imagined none of them had expected to hear this news tonight. He wasn't looking at her anymore, or her colleagues and their families. His eyes were on Mr. Blanderley and his friends. The men who owned the building they were all standing in.

Who *had* owned it. Who had sold it to Mr. Leith. Mr. Mordecai Leith, whose voice grinded on, emotionless and implacable.

"But this is, after all, the time of year for ringing out the old. Commercial leaseholders have already been notified. Notices to other tenants will go out over the next week. Demolition of the entire building will begin—"

Peony's ears rang. "Demolition? But I live here!"

She didn't realize she'd spoken aloud until everyone's eyes swung towards her.

Including his.

His eyes were like someone had taken the night sky and turned it into polished stone. Piercing and black and pitiless. They widened, slightly, as he looked down at her, and she hated how much she still found him the sexiest person she'd ever laid eyes on.

He was about to destroy her entire life, and all she wanted to do was kiss him.

2

Mordecai

Mordecai's whole life had built towards this moment: destroying the Hypatia.

He hadn't been prepared to meet his mate here.

His dragon recognized her immediately. It was in raptures. It wanted him to whisk her away that moment. It didn't understand why he wasn't doing so.

The answer was simple.

Perhaps if he'd spoken to her before he took that asshole Blanderley's invitation to address the crowd—the opportunity he'd been waiting for, *working* for, for so many years . . . but no. The moment was gone.

And the look in her eyes now wasn't love. It was shock. Confusion. And—*there it is*—hatred.

A muttered aside from Blanderley: "Ignore her. She's unimportant."

His dragon whipped around, ready to snap the man's head from his shoulders for daring to call his mate *unimportant*. It should have aimed its anger at Mordecai, instead. He kept talking, as though his tongue was on a conveyer belt. Timelines. Deadlines. The inexorable countdown towards the day the building and everything inside it would be nothing but rubble.

But the vicious glee he'd started his speech with was gone. Victory tasted like ashes. Yes, the old familiar faces had been horrified as he laid his plans bare. He'd laid his trap well. All those piecemeal agreements he'd made with the building's owners now meant that he had a controlling interest in the site. They'd lost control over the Hypatia, and try as they might to hide it—Blanderley even inviting him up onto the stage as though he knew all about his plans and hadn't discovered them only a moment before—they were as horrified as he had hoped.

But so was she.

But I live here. Her words echoed in his head. She lived here. She worked here. And he'd just told her he was going to destroy her life.

By the time he'd finished talking, the mood was crushed. Partygoers who'd started the evening happy and laughing drifted away alone or in whispering clumps. His mate was caught in the middle, a river stone battered by passing twigs and fallen leaves but unmoved by the rush of water. People farewelled her with smiles on their faces, but shot suspicious sidelong glances at her as they left.

He caught their whispers: Had she known about this? Why had she wasted their time talking about next year when the shop wasn't even going to exist? She'd promised them extra shifts, training, raises after the next budget was approved—what was the point of that if she knew they were all going to be jobhunting in the new year?

His chest tightened. *They'll hate her. This isn't how it was meant to be.*

He charged towards where he'd last seen her—and she was gone, all that was left a wisp of floral perfume. He whirled around, and fucking Blanderley was in his face. Of all the people he least wanted to see.

"That went over like a cup of old sick," Blanderley said. A day ago, an hour ago, Mordecai would have gloated over the hollow jollity in his voice. Now he just wished the man would go away. "Join us for a drink? Managers only. Figure maybe we could talk about . . . your announcement just now."

There it was. The flash of desperation in Blanderley's eyes. He'd been waiting for that flash for twenty years. It only lasted an instant, until the bastard convinced himself that he and the others could talk him around. Apply a little pressure. Make everything turn out for the best—*their* best—again.

This is what I want. Remember? Even their attempts to change his mind over drinks in God knew what sleazy club. He wanted to see them lose hope as he drank whatever top-shelf hock they plied him with.

But he needed to talk to his mate first. Explain himself.

What exactly am I going to explain to her?

I've taken everything from you, and I can't give it back. Not without losing everything I've worked for.

Scales rippled over his arms. He clenched his jaw, forcing them back. "You can take your drinks and—"

"What's this I hear about a managers' outing? *I'm* a manager. Why is this—?"

He turned.

She was there. His nostrils flared, and his tongue pressed

against the back of his teeth, all his senses trying to drink her in at once.

It was her eyes that caught him. They were fierce and glittering. And desperate. His chest wrenched. He wanted to see desperation in *their* eyes. Not hers.

Her throat bobbed as she came to a stop in front of him and Blanderley. God save him, she was facing him like he was a one-man firing squad. Spine rigid. Shoulders squared off. Chin thrust out. Only the repeated catch in her throat betrayed her. "Why is this the first I'm hearing about it?"

Blanderley gestured placatingly. "I'm afraid, Miss Fisher, this isn't that sort of—"

"Great!" Her voice was brittle. "I'll join you."

Her boss inclined his head. *Playing the kindly patriarch.* Mordecai's hackles rose. "My dear . . . Someone needs to clean up from the party."

Anger flared behind the desperation in her eyes. He could almost imagine her saying, *Clean up? When the whole building's condemned?* But out loud, her voice was perfectly chirpy and professional. "I haven't forgotten. Let me know where you're headed, and I'll meet you there."

Her whole body was radiating brittleness. And she hadn't so much as glanced at him since she stepped up to them.

Blanderley sighed. "All right, all right. But it's at Club Inferno. You'll need to—" He waved at her outfit. "They expect people to make an effort."

"There's nothing wrong with how Miss Fisher looks," Mordecai growled. Not for Club Inferno of all places.

She glanced at him—sudden, electric. Wings threatened to unfurl from his shoulders.

And what? Wrap around her? So I can carry her off to my lair? Hissing at Blanderley like an angry cat as I whisk her away?

He wouldn't do any of that. Because that would require breaking eye contact with her, and he couldn't bear to lose her gaze for even a second.

She tried to look away, and her eyes widened as she realized she couldn't. *She's as stuck as I am.*

Which meant she must recognize the bond between them.

Is she a shifter? he asked his dragon. He couldn't see anything other behind her eyes, the usual cue that someone was hiding an inner animal, but his dragon was more attuned than he was.

Almost, his dragon said.

What do you mean, almost?

It didn't matter. Because the next moment, she *wrenched* her gaze away and plastered on a smile. "Great! I'll tidy up and see you there."

Her spine was too rigid as she walked away. She could not have rejected him more clearly if she'd spat the words in his face.

Blanderley and his cronies offered him curt nods as they left. They had cars waiting outside—but no offers of a lift were forthcoming. Not from this lot. They would wait to confront him in private.

Not one of them bothered to farewell his mate.

"Miss Fisher—"

"Do I need to order you a taxi?" Her smile was still in place. But the brittle edge of her self-control was crumbling.

He cursed himself and tried a placating smile of his own. It rested unfamiliarly on his lips. "Miss Fisher. We weren't properly introduced." He held out his hand to her, and she stared at it like it was a knife. "Mordecai Leith."

"Yes, I *heard* your name, when Mr. Bl—" She cut herself off with a frustrated noise. He strongly suspected that the smile she was wearing was one she saved for particularly irritating customers. "Peony. Peony Fisher."

"Penny?"

"Peony. Like the flower."

"I didn't know there were flowers called peonies."

She colored and looked away. "Well. There are."

"They must be beautiful."

Her eyes met his, wide with astonishment. *Is this actually going well?* he dared to think.

Too soon.

Something flared in her gaze, bright and fiery and sharp—and then her eyes shuttered.

"I don't have time for this," she muttered. "I can't . . . not *now*, please. Will you just go? I can get you a taxi, an Uber, whatever you want."

"No need." His voice crackled with ice. "I won't bother you any further."

The store's big double doors swung shut behind him as he stalked off.

Rejected.

It happened. He had little to do with local shifter communities, but his grandmother had stories. The way she told it, their whole family would have been better off if she had rejected her own matebond. If his parents had never met. If he had never existed.

Was it any surprise that his mate would find him lacking, too?

What are you doing? his dragon asked, trying to make him look back over his shoulder at his mate. *Why are you leaving her?*

You heard her. She wants nothing to do with us. She— Stop that. We have to keep walking. His dragon kept an iron grip on his legs. Frustration lanced through his veins. *Are you doing this because I never shift into dragon form? You're taking over my body now?*

You're leaving her!

I'm saving us both from more heartbreak, he snapped. *You heard her. She lives and works at the Hypatia. I'm here to destroy it. There is no possible world in which this ends happily.* His breath puffed out in wild plumes of white vapor, almost as though he was breathing smoke.

What if we didn't destroy the Hypatia? his dragon suggested.

An old wound tugged inside him, so deep and hidden he'd forgotten he'd ever had it. Or how deep it had been to leave such a scar. *This is our life's work. Our purpose. Our family's revenge on the people who betrayed us.* He breathed out another long, slow plume of vapor. *Would you like to explain to Grandmother why we failed?*

No, it said hurriedly.

Well, then. His shoulders sagged.

So much for his moment of victory.

Let's go, he told it. *I have the papers in my pocket for the rest of those assholes to sign and get this whole sorry thing over with. There's no point in delaying.*

His legs still refused to move.

Dragon, he snarled in warning.

She's still there, it said.

And if she sees me standing out here? You think that being caught lurking will make this any better?

There was no way he could explain himself to her. The reasons he had for what he was doing had been part of his life for so long he wasn't sure he could put words to them anymore. He knew he was the villain in this story. He was the villain in every story. What else was he meant to be?

As for his inner dragon, and the magic that made him and Miss Fisher soulmates . . .

Peony. Peony Fisher. His beautiful mate, who smelled of flowers.

And who had so thoroughly rejected him, she wouldn't even acknowledge the connection between them. He'd felt it the moment he set eyes on her, but she acted as though she felt nothing.

Maybe this was for the best. After tonight, he would know he had a mate. He would know who she was. And he would know he would never have a chance with her. It gave certainty to something that had always been a question in his life.

With the Christmas lights twinkling above and the smell of snow on the air, he tried to tell himself it had only been a question. Not a desire. Not a heartsick longing for a connection that was the stuff of dreams.

He pulled out his phone, intending to check the most efficient route to the meeting location, and instead found himself searching for images of flowers. Peonies. They looked like roses, but infinitely wilder and more sumptuous.

He wondered what they smelled like. He wondered if they were what *she* smelled like.

Damn it. He shoved his phone back into his pocket.

You can't just leave her.

He clutched his forehead. *All this time I thought you were a logical creature*, he told his dragon. *I'll make sure she's not left on the street when the Hypatia comes down.* His stomach twisted. *Whatever happens.*

What about the drinks?

He made a frustrated noise. *We're not going to see her at drinks. You heard the others. They never intended her to join them at all. If she turns up on her own, they won't let her through the door.*

And you're just going to let that happen?

His shoulders stiffened as he tried to find a way to explain himself to his dragon. The situation was too complicated. Peony would be in enough difficulties without him taking her to the board meeting like some sort of cursed fairy godmother.

And he didn't want to see her face as he stripped the last of her hope away.

You're a coward, his dragon told him.

He set his jaw. *It's the best option for both of us.*

Coward. You'd rather hide than tell her the truth!

Then I'm a villain and a coward, he told it. *So be it.*

At last his dragon seemed to get the message. His legs

unlocked. He stalked off. There were taxis on the street, but he needed the sharpness of icy air in his lungs. He would walk until the Hypatia was out of sight, and then—

Idiot, his dragon said, and tangled his feet under him.

He landed on his back. All the wind was knocked out of him, and he flailed, inelegantly, more like a turtle than a dragon shifter. He'd hit his shoulder on the edge of the sidewalk—the pain radiated along his arm and back up to his neck, then took a detour to meet its new friend-pains in his hip and twisted ankle. He hissed in a breath and snarled out a curse.

"What is the point of having you around if you can't even stop me taking a fall like that?" The pain made him forget that normal people didn't talk out loud to the voices in their heads.

A face appeared above him, haloed in light from one of the few unbroken streetlights. It was her. Oh god and little fishes, of course it was her. She'd pulled a bulky coat over her clothes and her face was half-hidden behind its furred hood, but there was no mistaking his mate.

So much for running away from her, his dragon said smugly.

She looked like an angel.

"I should leave you here to freeze," she said.

The look of shock had disappeared from her face. The desperation, too. Which should have been a good sign, except for what had replaced it: she was looking at him as though he was a smear of something unsavory she'd almost trodden on.

Or—he took in the narrowed eyes and the thinned line of her mouth—like something she *wanted* to tread on.

Ahhhh, cried his dragon. *Our mate! She came for us!*

3

PEONY

Peony had been so busy glaring at Mordecai and telling herself how super not attracted to him she was that it took her a moment to realize what she was seeing. He stalked off—*not sexily*, she told herself. *There's nothing sexy about the back of his head or his shoulders or the ass he's hiding under his stupid coat.*

Then his feet went out from under him.

He landed heavily.

And didn't get back up.

Shit.

If that prick Poor-Little-Matchgirls himself on Christmas Eve outside my shop . . . She didn't know what would happen to the sale of the Hypatia if the new owner froze to death in the snow, but the narrow chance that it would mean happy-ever-after for the bookstore wasn't worth the bad publicity. She threw on her coat and hurried over.

The look on his face when he saw her leaning over him was almost enough to make her head straight back inside. He met her eyes as though she were the last person on the planet he wanted to see.

"I should leave you here to freeze," she said.

"Very likely," he gritted out.

"Lucky for you, I have a better plan."

His eyebrows went up. She tried not to show that she was surprised, too.

But this was her one chance to do something about the disaster her life had become. She couldn't let it slip through her fingers.

"Come on," she said, holding out a gloved hand to him. "Let me help you up. And then, you're going to take me out for drinks."

A flash of something—*Interest? Suspicion?*—glinted in his eyes. It was intoxicating. She wanted to keep doing this: wrongfoot him, surprise him, take him off his guard.

Then he reached for her hand, and she was the one taken off-guard.

She leaned forward at the same moment he reached up, and instead of taking her hand, he grasped her around her bare wrist. His touch was suddenly, shockingly intimate. His hand disappearing into the sleeve of her coat. Skin to skin.

He leapt up like the icy sidewalk had burned him, and snatched his hand away.

Peony swayed as he released her. Swayed *towards* him, as though he were an ocean current drawing her in. "I . . ."

"Excuse me." He grabbed his own hand as though it was burning, too, and hunted out a pair of leather gloves from his pockets. She should have been outraged. Yes. Outrage was the feeling she should have been feeling. It was there, waiting in the wings for its big moment. But it would have to keep waiting.

He looked as shocked as she felt. His black, broken-glass

eyes were wide under their necromancer eyebrows. As though touching her *had* been something intimate. Something shocking. Something...

Her heart flipped over.

Frog, she reminded herself. *And he looks like he's about to find a handy lily pad to hide under.*

She grabbed his arm before he could scuttle away.

He stared at her, dazed. "Drinks? You followed me out here to ask me on a date?"

The vague expression left his eyes. The expression that replaced it was hideously familiar. She'd seen it at the end of every date she'd ever been on. As if she'd needed to hear them reject her to know things weren't going to work. One kiss was all she needed to figure that out.

"Ask you out? No. You're my ticket to whatever old boys' club party Blanderley and his friends are having." She drew herself up. "I should have received an invitation. I'm a manager, too. *And* a resident. I—I should be involved in any decision-making."

Her voice did not wobble on the last bit. Not at all. Well. Maybe a tiny bit. She forced her eyes away from Mordecai before she saw whether he noticed.

"I see." Mordecai straightened his shoulders. His biceps flexed under her fingers. "Are you sure that's a good idea?"

"That's none of your concern. You're just my ticket inside." His eyebrows shot up. "Don't look so shocked. And don't worry. I'll let go of you as soon as you take me to wherever you're all meeting up."

Her throat tightened. *Blanderley is going to hate this. But what's the worst that can happen? I lose my job and my apartment in one fell swoop? Double-fired and double-homeless?*

"Very well." Mordecai looked down his nose at her. It should have been enraging. It should *not* have made her think inappropriate thoughts about repressed librarians.

I'm a bookseller! If anyone here is a repressed book-adjacent person, it should be me!

Mordecai sighed heavily. "Fine. I'll hail a cab."

Because we mere peasantry are incapable of such a thing. Sure. You go ahead. She hooked her arm around his and turned towards the street. "So, Club *Inferno*? Honestly, I wouldn't have thought it of Mr. Blanderley. He's always struck me as more of the sherry-and-cigarettes type."

Mordecai muttered something, took a step with her—and his leg collapsed under him. His weight fell against her, and they half-tripped, half-stumbled to catch their balance together.

"Are you all right?" She stared into his white-lipped face. "Is it your leg? You should have said something!"

"And interrupt your scheming? Heaven forbid." A whisper of a smile flashed across his face.

Peony stared. Was he *joking* with her?

And worse . . . did she like it?

Oh god. I do like it.

She sniffed. "Thank you. My scheming must not be interrupted. But if you're that badly hurt . . ."

"It's nothing." He tried to put weight on his foot again and winced. "It *shouldn't* be a problem. Why haven't you healed it already?"

The last sentence was muttered in an angry undertone. She got the distinct impression she wasn't meant to hear it. In fact, she would have bet he meant to say it inside his head, not out loud, except that the pain he was trying not to show on his face had overridden his plans.

"I'm very much afraid," he said, straightening with a look of disgust, "that before I take you anywhere, I'm going to have to request your help again."

"You didn't ask for it before," she pointed out.

"Then let me throw myself on your mercy without falling to the ground this time," he countered through gritted teeth. Oh, hell, he really was in pain. Peony took a deep breath.

You can do this. It's not that much different to holding on to his arm.

She wrapped one arm around his waist and put her shoulder beneath his.

His coat wasn't bulky and padded like hers. It was slim-fitting and probably made from the wool of sheep genetically modified to be both fashionable and extra insulating while still leaving her in no doubt of the shape of the body beneath it. Her cheeks flooded with heat. The arm she'd wrapped around him felt too warm. Other parts of her anatomy woke up with an excited tingle like they wanted the chance to heat up, too.

Oh god.

She cleared her throat. "Fine. Come on, let's get your ankle iced." She maneuvered him around, and together, they limped back to the Hypatia.

They were in the elevator when Mordecai finally realized

she wasn't taking him back into the bookstore. "Where are we going?"

"The first-aid kit at the store is good for paper cuts, less good for sprains." She hesitated. Telling him felt like taking off a piece of armor.

What? That makes no sense. What's so revealing about telling him that not only is he going to destroy your work, he's going to leave you homeless, as well?

Oh, right. *That* was why it felt like baring her secrets to him. Because it meant he would know exactly how much power he held over her.

Should have left him to freeze.

"We're heading to my apartment," she said shortly.

The words seemed to take a moment to penetrate his brain. She could live with that. Waiting for his reaction gave her something to worry about. Something that wasn't—to take an example entirely at random—the fact that their bodies were literally rubbing against each other.

Through several layers of clothes, but still. Rubbing.

I am going to die. Right here. He isn't even going to get a chance to demolish the building. It's going to burn down from the fire caused by how turned on I am right now.

They took the elevator—which was working, thank goodness—and got out on her floor.

"I'm just down here," she said, pointing.

"Your apartment." Mordecai's voice was flat. "You live here."

"Oh, you didn't hear me tell the whole party before? Yes. Since I got my first paycheck after graduation."

He cursed. Not even under his breath. Then he stopped walking, which meant Peony had to stop walking, too, or he would probably fall over or something. His eyes searched hers, quick and assessing. She resisted the urge to hide.

What are you looking at me like that for? You're the one who came in here to ruin everything!

"Don't go to meet the others for drinks tonight." There was a note of urgency in his voice that made her hackles rise.

"Why not?"

"It'll only make things worse."

"What things?" She threw up her hands, releasing him, and he stumbled and caught his balance against the wall. "Will I get double-fired? Double-thrown-out-of-my-apartment?"

"I don't want you to be hurt."

He took her hand. She froze. What was going on? Why was she so affected by him? He was hot, yes, but he was an asshole. He was destroying her life. And now he was looking at her like he felt bad for her?

That was even worse.

I have to stop this.

"You don't want me to be hurt? So, you're going to, what, *not* tear down the Hypatia?"

A tinny Christmas carol chimed from her pocket. *Not Mom again. Please . . .* She declined the call without taking her eyes off Mordecai's face.

"No."

"Then why keep bringing it up?" She wasn't sure what had her more on edge: the expression on Mordecai's face or waiting to find out if her mother was going to keep calling and calling until she finally picked up.

Her phone stayed silent. She still felt like she was standing on the edge of a cliff. Great. That answered *that* question.

She raised her hands in surrender. "I'm sorry. I don't know why you'd care, anyway. Let's just . . . Look. I've got ice in here for your ankle." They were outside her apartment. She unlocked the door and barged in without waiting for him to respond.

Not that there was much space to barge around in. Once upon a time, the Hypatia's apartments had been elegant suites of rooms. Cue a half-hearted development twenty or so years ago, and the elegant suites had been chopped up into bedsits that barely fit a bed, let alone anywhere to sit.

"You live here," Mordecai said again, and she bristled.

"Again. *Yes.* Are you sure you didn't hit your head as well as fall on your ass?"

Who are you? she squeaked internally. *Where did all this attitude come from?* She felt like a maiden aunt staring in horror at her scandalous young charge, who was also her.

Maybe she'd hit her head, too.

"Excuse me," she said primly. "Take a seat. I'll grab the ice."

She squeezed into what her landlord—one of Blanderley's friends—insisted was a kitchenette and grabbed a bag of frozen vegetables from the tiny fridge-freezer. When she turned around, Mordecai had just realized that his only seating option was her bed.

She took exquisite delight in the uncomfortable look on his face. "Make yourself at home," she said breezily. He sat, stiff-legged and straight-shouldered, like he was about to face a firing squad as she knelt in front of him. "Which ankle was it?"

"You don't need to— Yes, it's that one."

Frog, she reminded herself as she folded up the leg of his pants to bare his shin. *Necromancer. Evil wizard. Every villainous count from every Gothic horror novel.*

But he had really nice legs.

"Good news, this barely looks swollen at all," she told him.

"Is that good news?" he muttered under his breath.

"Most people would think so." She had to stop staring at his ankle. Right. Now.

She looked up into his face instead, and that was worse.

She was kneeling between his legs. There wasn't enough room for her to kneel anywhere else, but there it was. He was sitting with his legs apart, this huge dark crow of a man with eyes like splintered glass, whose expression of frustration only made him more goddamned attractive to her, somehow, and she was on her knees in front of him. His coat had fallen open over his legs. She followed the seam of his pants up to a telltale bulge.

The bag of frozen vegetables in her hand wouldn't last a second, pressed against her blazing cheeks.

Deep breaths, Peony.

She inhaled, and Mordecai's glittering eyes dropped from her face to her chest.

She was still wearing her party dress. It didn't show much, but apparently that didn't matter.

Hell, no one had looked at her like that before, even when

she *wasn't* wearing clothes. Which hadn't been often—she kept to a catch-and-release policy when it came to kissing frogs—but . . . still.

Mordecai's throat worked. His eyes were back on her face, and something hungry passed behind them. "Miss Fisher—"

"Don't *Miss Fisher* me. The least you could do is call me by my first name as you ruin my life."

"I have no intention of ruining your life."

"You could have fooled me!" His ankle wasn't just *barely* swollen. It wasn't swollen at all. Was he even hurt?

"You clearly don't want to hear it, but regardless of your own feelings on the matter, I will not pretend it doesn't exist."

What was he talking about now?

"You won't be left homeless. I have other properties around the city. You can have your pick of apartments."

"Is this an offer you'll be making all the residents or only the ones kneeling between your legs?"

His face went white, with a slash of red across his cheeks. "That isn't— I don't— *What* other residents?"

Peony's jaw set. He wanted to play dirty? Remind her that she was practically the only person who still rented here?

Because even the promotion to manager didn't come with enough of a raise to move anywhere else, a treacherous voice in her head said. *Because you thought living here was some grand romantic adventure while you waited for your real life to begin, not a place you'd be stuck into your thirties while everyone else moved on.*

Her chest ached, and suddenly she wasn't upset—she was angry. Why did he have to come here and turn her life upside down? Why had she gone after him, of all stupid ideas, and brought him back to her room like an injured bird?

An injured evil crow, she thought. *Or . . . or a bat. Something big, with wings and . . . scales . . .*

She shook her head. What she *really* wanted was to put him off-balance again. To provoke that expression of shock—and had she imagined the moment of naked longing before he locked himself away again behind that prissy scowl?

That. More of that.

"If you don't want any special treatment, that can be arranged," Mordecai said. Through gritted teeth. *Actually* through gritted teeth. "I'll offer everyone the same terms."

"That's very fair of you."

"Let me make one thing clear." He leaned forward, his broken-glass eyes piercing her. "I am *not* doing this out of a sense of fairness."

It was like she was in a play but had forgotten her script. She had no idea what was going on. But the heat in his eyes left her breathless, and her body was making little encouraging noises—okay, *big* encouraging noises—and everything else had gone wrong, so . . .

What the hell. One more bad decision couldn't make this night any worse.

She grabbed his face between her hands and kissed him.

His lips were soft. Somehow, she'd expected them to be sharp, like his eyes.

The taste of him shot straight through her. She wanted more. She wanted to lick him all over. No, she wanted to *tell* him she wanted to lick him all over, and make his face burn with shocked lust all over again. And then do it.

She was sure the last frog she'd kissed hadn't muddled her mind like this.

She wanted—

I want him to kiss me back.

His lips were soft, but the rest of him was rigid with shock. The Peony she recognized—the one who did not maul random evil wizards—emerged slowly as though from a great mental depth. *Oh.*

Maybe this wasn't just a bad decision. Maybe it was a terrible decision.

Then he let out a shuddering gasp. His mouth opened beneath hers. He kissed her deeply, savagely. She was vaguely aware of his body unstiffening. Was he going to put his arms around her? Oh god, she wanted him to hold her.

She—

The ruffled-restless-mischievous feeling inside her flared to life. Everything went blurry.

The next minute, she was staring at Mordecai's shoes.

What?

She looked down, and her vision whirled. Not only was the floor a lot closer than it had been a second ago, but those weren't her feet. They were *paws*. Fuzzy, sand-colored paws. Her nose twitched; a thousand, thousand smells crashed into her senses, and *whiskers* trembled at the edges of her vision.

Oh no. Oh no no no no.

The tree-trunk-like columns of Mordecai's legs bent. He

knelt in front of her, his face pale with shock, his eyes like chips of distilled and frozen midnight. "Peony?"

He ran one hand across his face. Shock gave his face more life than she'd seen on it yet.

The shock gave way to something softer. Tentative. He lowered his hand.

Peony?

His lips didn't move, but his voice rolled through her mind. Her hair—her *fur*—stood on end. Telepathy was one of the shifter abilities she'd missed out on so far in her life.

Wait.

She could hear Mordecai's voice in her head because she was a shifter. He could speak telepathically . . . because he was, too.

She had found her soulmate.

And it was Mordecai Leith.

He knew, she thought suddenly. He was a shifter. He must have recognized her as his mate when he first saw her.

And he'd tried to leave. Without saying anything to her. If he hadn't slipped on the ice . . .

She stared up into his dark eyes, and he looked . . . resigned.

She really hadn't thought she had any heart left to break. But she was learning so many things about herself tonight. What was one more?

4

MORDECAI

Mordecai had no idea what the hell he was meant to do.

First his mate had rejected him. Then she'd kissed him. And now, just as he'd clawed himself back from the delicious shock of her lips against his, she'd shifted?

It's one way of showing she's having second thoughts.

He straightened his shoulders, which was the opposite of what his dragon wanted to do. It wanted to lie down at her feet and roll over so she could pet his belly. Which was not a feeling he'd previously associated with his dragon. Ever.

Then again, it had never tripped him and put him flat on his back, either.

"You're a shifter too," he began, schooling his voice so it came out neutral. Too neutral. He tried again. "That's—"

No, Peony-the-cat groaned, burying her face in her paws. *No, no, no. How can this be happening?*

"You've transformed," he said dryly, then frowned. *Does she really not know what is happening?*

If this was the first time she'd shifted . . . if she didn't even know what shifters were—

She didn't reject us, after all? his dragon suggested.

He made a sharp, negatory gesture. A muscle in his cheek

twitched. *Then fate has chosen the worst possible moment for it. I am the last person anyone would want to help nursemaid them through the revelation that magic exists.*

He sighed briskly. "Has this not happened to you before? Some people have the ability to—"

No! I know what shifters are! But it isn't meant to happen like this! She lashed her tail and let out a pained yowl. *This means . . . it means . . .*

Her telepathic voice was raw. She didn't even try to hide her emotions, and they stampeded down their psychic connection. Disgust. Horror. Fear. And a sense of rib-tightening helplessness.

He tried again. "Is this the first time you've shifted?"

She went completely still. *N-no? Wait. You're hearing me? You're hearing me when I'm like this?*

All shifters are able to communicate telepathically with one another. He sounded like he was reciting from an informational leaflet.

I know that! She reared up on her back legs, tottered sideways, and fell back onto all fours. *I—I . . . it's a shock, that's all. I . . . haven't done this in a while.*

Nor have I. He tried to smile. From the way Peony-the-cat's ears went back, it was unsuccessful.

I'm not very good at it. Her tail twitched. *Can we, um . . . Can you hear if I say . . .* Her voice went muffled in his head.

Not quite.

Oh thank god, if he heard what I actually thought about him, I'd— YOU HEARD THAT? YOU CAN HEAR THAT?

What had given it away? Mordecai's jaw twitched. "Yes."

Okay. Well. Shit. Sorry. You heard that too?

He nodded.

Something that sounded very much like a wail of frustration echoed through his head.

Sorry. Sorry! This is all just . . . a lot. I didn't, um . . . I didn't mean to shift just now. This is . . . awkward.

"We're in agreement about that, at least."

And you're— Her voice fell ominously silent.

"I can understand why you wanted to avoid this conversation," Mordecai said stiffly. Quiet swearing echoed at the edges of his mind. The tiny sandy-colored cat rubbed its face agitatedly. "I am sorry to have put you in this position."

YOU'RE sorry? Because I wanted to avoid— Oh. Right. I get it. But . . . you're my mate. I'm your— Okay. This is okay.

Mordecai had the distinct impression that 'okay' wasn't the word she'd intended to use.

His stomach clenched. "Miss Fisher—"

. . . Seriously? The little cat blinked at him as though he'd lost his mind. *If the last time I said this didn't stick, I think we can cut the formalities now. My name's Peony. You might as well use it.*

"Peony." Unbidden, a profusion of flowers burst into his mind. Pink and orange and red, voluptuous blooms that blazed like sunset but were cool and soft against the skin. Her skin. Which would be even softer, if her lips were anything to go by. Soft and sweet and . . .

He hauled his thoughts back into order. "We need to decide what to do next."

Next as in right now, or next as in . . .? Her mental voice disintegrated into a buzz of confused half-thoughts. But he got the message.

Next as in the rest of our lives.

They were true mates. For whatever reason, the universe had decided that they were each other's perfect pair. So why did the emotion welling inside him feel like dread, not joy?

"This would be easier if you were in your human form."

Would it? She fell silent again.

He flicked a quick glance at Peony-the-cat. She was sitting staring at nothing. *Either she's figured out how to keep her thoughts private, or she's so traumatized by the thought of being my mate that her brain has turned to static.*

For the second time that night, he wanted to run away. Like a coward. He cleared his throat. "The board are expecting me."

She looked at him like she couldn't believe what she was hearing. He didn't blame her.

"You obviously need time to come to terms with . . . this." *Us.*

Are you kidding me right now, you absolute prick?

He winced.

Oh fuck fuck fuck, he heard that.

"And I deserved it." Oh, fantastic. Now he sounded like a *magnanimous* prick. "Let me take you somewhere you can relax and think things over. I'll attend the board meeting and meet you afterwards."

The hell you will! Peony pounced. Tiny claws pierced his jacket as she scrambled up his chest until she was glaring straight into his face.

Hee, his dragon grinned. It rustled its wings, ready to rear up and display itself in response to its mate's approach.

Absolutely not. He wrestled it back. The last thing he needed was to terrify his mate more by showing her the creature he kept locked away inside him.

Peony-the-cat glared at him. He fought the urge to grab hold of her. Not to pull her off his jacket or move her, just to touch her. As though his touch could fix anything.

"If you were in your human form—"

It wouldn't make a difference, would it? You already told me not to bother going.

"Why haven't you shifted back?"

She stared at him. The gold in her eyes rose up as her claws sliced deeper into his lapels. Her fluffy sides heaved. *I . . . I don't want to.*

She's lying, his dragon said, confused. *Why is she lying?*

It wouldn't take much to find out why. If he spoke to her mind-to-mind, rather than insisting on this one-sided out-loud dialogue, it would be easier for him to sense her feelings along with her words.

But that would require an intimacy he wasn't ready for yet.

What? You talk to other shifters like that all the time! his dragon protested.

Yes. Shifters he was facing across the negotiating table or manipulating by edging their thoughts with fear of the dragon lurking inside him. Not his mate. Not the woman he was meant to treasure, not terrify.

As though I haven't done that already. That must be why she was stuck in her animal form. The shock of finding out he was her mate had been too much.

I should have let her go.

"Tell me what you need." He tried to make his voice gentle. The tiny cat stared at him suspiciously. "Whatever you need to help you take human form again. And then we can discuss . . . *this* further. Stay here, if you prefer. You can't go anywhere like this."

That's where you're wrong. Tiny claws flexed through his merino suit jacket and the cotton shirt beneath to prick into his skin. **You're going to take me to the board meeting. And because you're my mate, once you're there, you're going to say you've changed your mind about destroying the Hypatia.**

I must be mad.

The logical thing to do would have been to leave Peony back at the building, or, better yet, take her to his home, where she would be safe, and attend the function alone. Enjoy his victory and then deal with his mate. In that order.

Instead, he was ferrying her around in his jacket pocket like some sort of sharp-clawed Christmas elf.

He was mad. Clearly.

But the idea of leaving her in the Hypatia, pretending so hard she wasn't so overwhelmed that she couldn't even control her shifting, left him with a pit in his stomach. And as for taking her home—

He never took anyone home. Normally, he told himself this was because it was his sanctuary. The one place he could be free of the bullshit that dogged the rest of his life.

For some reason, when he thought of bringing her there, his luxurious apartment felt as cold and dim as the matchbox-sized excuse for an apartment his mate lived in.

And as if that wasn't bad enough . . .

You have it the wrong way around, his dragon insisted with a derisory puff of smoke. *You should deal with your victory, and then enjoy your mate.*

You are not helping, he told it sternly.

What? I have already helped a great deal. Remember when I made you fall over?

Mordecai gritted his teeth. *Unfortunately.*

Enjoy Peony? The thought tore at him. She was so full of life and fervor, and he was . . . himself. *If the world were different . . . If I were a different man . . . If I'd made different choices . . .*

Except his choices hadn't been choices at all. They were his fate, the same as she was. One he'd pursued like a hunter chasing its quarry, with no time for anything else. And now she was here, in his life where he'd left no room for her.

Where are we? Her voice skittered nervously against his mind, and he repressed a sudden urge to pat the pocket she was hiding in.

"Outside the club. You can't hear it?" He wasn't concerned about anyone overhearing his one-sided conversation; outside the club, they would assume he was talking on the phone. Inside, it would take a shifter's enhanced senses to have any chance of hearing him.

I can hear lots of things. And smell lots of things. She sounded amazed. *Is this what it's always like? Um. Here, I mean. I'm not a big club person.*

Neither was he. But his dragon offered him a vision of Peony in the skimpy clothes favored by most of the men and women waiting to be let inside.

She would be very cold, it suggested. *You would have to find a way to warm her up.*

If he gritted his teeth any harder, they were going to shatter. "I have no idea what it's like to have a cat's senses."

Tiny claws pricked the lining of his jacket. *Thanks for rubbing it in. What's it like for whatever amazing creature you can turn into, then? The one that was so incredible you couldn't show me back at the shop?* She paused and then added, *The GIANT ASSHOLE animal. Giantus Assholius.*

He was fairly certain she hadn't meant to say that last part out loud.

"My animal's sensory input is different, but it soon becomes second nature." He hesitated. "Or so I expect. Like you, I don't spend a great deal of time in my animal form."

Not like me. Her voice was tiny and not meant for him, but it cut like a knife. So much for attempting to find common ground.

Club Inferno's entranceway was as obvious as its name. Gilt Greek-style arch and columns, red velvet, and a crowd of would-be revelers wearing inappropriately little clothing for the icy weather. All it needed was flames licking around the bases of the columns and the scene would be perfectly set.

He stalked closer and winced. Not flames: Christmas lights. Cheerful, twinkly stars and miniature candy-canes everywhere he looked.

Christmas in Hell. How appropriate.

He marched past the crowded queue. There were two bouncers at the door; he nodded curtly at the nearest one and kept walking. The second bouncer frowned and moved to intercept him, but his partner raised an arm to stop him. Their whispered conversation followed him as far as the first blast of sound from inside the club.

At least Santa's devils know to show some respect. It had been years since anyone stopped him from going exactly where he wanted, and he was damned if he'd break the streak for a place like Inferno.

Inside, the air was heavy with heat and the bass-thump of music and a strong, incongruous scent of peppermint and mixed spice. In his pocket, Peony sneezed.

Mordecai did his best to surreptitiously breathe through his mouth and tried not to pay too much attention to the décor. He envied Peony, hidden in his pocket and not forced to absorb the club's idea of sexy Christmas decorations.

I can't believe I'm missing out on all of this, she complained. *It smells horrible! It sounds worse! What is the DJ doing to Mariah Carey?*

He had been putting some effort into ignoring the music, but let up long enough to hear what sounded like a wounded robot declaring that it was going to re-gift its heart to somebody else. Presumably a heart it had previously stolen from something warm-blooded.

He shuddered.

It's awful. I . . . oh no. I love it.

"I'm glad you're enjoying yourself," he muttered facetiously.

Thank you. I am. Needle-like claws found the skin above his hipbone with unerring accuracy. *Peppermint and nutmeg? Disgusting.*

"We agree on that."

I need to try it. What is it? Some sort of horrific bar snack?

Did she expect him to order whatever it was?

He passed the bar en-route to the VIP section. Oh god. *It's a drink.*

It's a DRINK? That's perfect. Order one! She sounded giddy. Was the sensory overload making her drunk? *Seriously, this is where Blanderley is holding the end-of-year drinks? I always thought they went somewhere upmarket for those. Peppermint and nutmeg mixers are not what I had in mind. But I'm willing to sacrifice my tastebuds in the name of research. Well. I'm a cat, which makes things tricky, so instead, I'm willing to sacrifice YOUR tastebuds.*

"I'm flattered," he said dryly.

Good.

"But I will absolutely not be ordering whatever that abomination is."

Spoilsport. Her voice buzzed like a radio slightly out of tune. *I can't believe I kissed him. Oh god. How could everything go so wrong?*

His spine stiffened. Not drunk, then. Buoying herself up

with ridiculousness because the alternative was admitting she was stuck with him.

But . . .

She came after me. He had left, and she had chased him. Yes, she was overwhelmed, and the discovery that her mate was the man who was about to destroy her livelihood must be difficult for her to come to terms with—good God, she was right, he really was an almighty prick, even inside his own thoughts—but *she had come after him.* She had seen that he was her mate, and, despite everything, she'd hunted him down.

She chose me.

It had to mean something.

Hope was an unfamiliar sensation for Mordecai. All his life, he'd aimed himself at his goals and done whatever it took to achieve them. Hope was irrelevant; he'd planned and taken action and won. Now, for the first time, he felt the uncertainty of an emotion he didn't know how to deal with.

"Leith!" One of the Hypatia owners waved at him from the top of the stairs that led to the VIP area.

Mordecai's face settled into its usual arrogant lines as he nodded a greeting to the other man. It was as familiar as pulling on his jacket. *Without* a cat in the pocket.

Uneasiness nipped at his heels as he headed for the stairs. If he'd only then pulled on his usual expression . . . *What expression was I making before now?*

Hope.

It felt dangerous.

5

PEONY

Peony's nose was twitching.

The *smells*.

Food and alcohol and floor polish and pine needles and *people*. So many people. So many *smelly* people. People who smelled of body wash and cologne and perfume and things they'd eaten earlier that day. And things they'd stepped in. Things they'd brushed past.

It was too much. Her eyes were watering. This had to be normal, right? For her animal. Not for her. She didn't know how she was meant to deal with the overload of sensory information.

Fight them!

And now her inner cat wanted her to fight the smells. Inner cat? Outer cat? It was too confusing. Why had she wanted to be here so much?

The Hypatia. Remember?

The Hypatia. Her prologue-job. Her prologue-apartment.

Except her prologue had just finished, hadn't it?

So why was she here, really?

Because her other option was seeing Mordecai leave.

Or not leave.

If he'd stayed, and she'd managed to shift back . . .

Her heart thudded. It was all too much, and coming here was seeming like more and more of a mistake. *Another* mistake. She concentrated, trying to narrow down her senses. The smell of peppermint and nutmeg and alcohol. The auditory torture of whatever Christmas carol had been sacrificed to create the noise blasting around them. The warmth of Mordecai's body through his jacket lining and, beneath the other smells and sounds but no less powerful, his masculine scent and the steady thrum of his heartbeat. The rumble in his chest when he spoke out loud or, more frequently, grumbled under his breath. The—

No. No no no. My super shifter senses are meant to distract *me from thinking about him. Not make him the only thing I can think about.*

Because thinking about him had almost made her shift, back at the apartment. There had been a moment, as she clung with her new needle-sharp claws to the front of his jacket, when she'd thought *What if I was grabbing him with my hands, instead*, and things had gotten . . . fuzzy.

Why had she stopped?

Why did I kiss him in the first place?

It was too late, anyway. If she thought about him too hard now? Here? Out in public?

"We're here. Are you sure about this? We can still leave."

Of course he wanted to leave. She'd used the matebond to threaten him into coming here and handing control of the Hypatia back to the board.

She couldn't let him leave before she'd gotten what she

wanted.

Even if every second she spent accidentally noticing how good Mordecai smelled or how he was so warm that it wouldn't even matter if she didn't have any clothes on when she shifted back, because—

No! No no no!

"Is everything alright?"

No! she blurted out. **I mean . . . yes! It's fine. Everything's fine. Let's go in now.** With her hiding in his pocket and definitely absolutely no way shifting back into human form because she'd thought too hard about how nice he smelled.

Oh god.

"Very well." He sounded doubtful. She didn't blame him.

And as if that wasn't bad enough . . .

We're sneaking! the squeaky voice in her head said. *Sneaking! Yes! Tell him we're sneaking!*

No.

Yes!

No! I'm not going to—

"Not going to what? Ah. That was another thing I wasn't meant to hear, wasn't it?"

She sighed. It came out an adorable squeak. **My . . . cat . . . is excited about sneaking in.**

"Is it always so dominant?"

Dominant? **Uh. Maybe?** She was subordinate to the fluffy kitten of her own soul. Great.

It's probably . . . Think of an excuse. Any excuse. **. . . meeting you. The shock? The . . . it's big. It's a lot.**

Was she imagining it, or did he briefly cup his hand around the tiny shape of her through his jacket? "It is."

She must have imagined it. Mordecai's gait changed as he began walking up the stairs. That was what she'd felt. Not him touching her.

He didn't even reach for me when I kissed him. The kiss that had ruined everything.

The frisky, mischievous feeling inside her from her cat faded. And suddenly it was a lot easier to ignore how good Mordecai smelled.

"Leith. There you are. Thought you'd never show up." One of the owners. Peony went completely still, except for every single hair on her body, which stood on end.

Oh. Right. *That* was why she was here.

"We're still waiting on Blanderley. Probably arguing with the driver over his fare, haw haw."

Ugh. She'd forgotten Hebbings made that noise. Like a laughing donkey.

"It wouldn't surprise me." Mordecai's voice was chilly. "Where's this private room? Or do you want to talk business where anyone could hear us?"

"We should wait for Blanderley—"

"He can't find the room on his own?"

"Leith's right. Come on, Arthur, my throat's dry. I need something to wash away that rubbish they served at the party."

"Party? Is that what you call it? I haven't been so bored in years."

Oh no. The board smelled *awful*. All of them. Peony covered her nose with her paws, trying to escape the cacophony of smells. To her horror, the one smell that wasn't attacking her nose like a swarm of stinky bees appeared to be . . . Mordecai.

He smelled of leather and wood smoke and something her cat decided, with a wriggle of delight, was *danger*.

The only danger I'm in is shifting during this meeting and winding up naked in front of my boss and all his horrible friends.

Maybe she should just stop breathing altogether.

"Peony? What was that about shifting in front of your boss?"

Why wouldn't he speak telepathically to her? Did the idea of reaching for her with his mind disgust him so much he was willing to risk the humans thinking he was talking nonsense to himself?

Nothing. Just an intrusive thought. Nothing's going to happen. On cue, her cat extended all of its claws and dug them into Mordecai's hipbone. He hissed in a breath. *Except you taking back what you said you'd do to the Hypatia.*

Mordecai drew a slow breath. Even in cat form, bombarded by sensations on all sides, she could tell how forbearing and patient a breath it was. Her stomach dipped. "Peony, you need to understand that—"

"There you are. The hell you all waiting around for out here? What, the room isn't ready yet?"

She would recognize her boss's voice anywhere. It was like a bucket of ice water on the thoughts that were threatening to make her shift.

"We were waiting to see if we'd have to send someone to haul you off that driver, haw haw."

"Bastard overcharged me. Thought he could get away with putting extra on the meter just because we parked in the congestion zone. Pah!"

"If you're all quite done?" Mordecai's voice was cold as ice. His displeasure was clear, and Peony sighed in relief. If he'd turned out to be the sort of asshole who bonded over fighting service workers for pennies . . . "I'd prefer to get this over with as fast as possible."

The roar of the club lessened as Mordecai walked through a pair of heavy double doors into what Peony assumed was the VIP lounge. She peeked out over the top of his pocket and glimpsed dark red leather couches and rancid-looking yellow lighting.

Yuck. I can't believe I always saw Blanderley and the rest of the board as more . . . classy.

Mordecai snorted. A shiver of pleasure went through her. "At least it shouldn't smell as bad back here."

You clearly can't smell your drinking buddies very well in human form. I'm going to need you to order one of those peppermint spice cocktails as a medicinal measure, she reminded him.

"I will not, and your sinuses may thank me for it."

She giggled, and he went stiff with surprise.

It took a few minutes for the board members to settle around what, by the smell and squeaky sound of it, was a leather-upholstered booth. A server came in to take their orders. Champagne popped, and the men sneered over the food options the same way they'd sneered over her catering.

Maybe it's a good thing I'm in cat form. I don't think I could stand this in human form. She knew she couldn't. Faced with the combined assholery of her boss and his friends, she would have wilted like week-old lettuce.

But Mordecai wouldn't. One look from his broken-glass eyes would quell them more effectively than any of her carefully written requests or spreadsheet-backed recommendations. And . . . surely they didn't *want* him to take over the building?

She just had to convince him to take her side and agree with the others that the Hypatia was fine the way it was, and everything would be fine.

We're going to convince him with our claws, right? her cat suggested.

Not with her claws.

Well, only as a last resort.

Mordecai sat, careful not to crush her, and she waited for the tension in the room to rise. Berwick would start it off, she guessed, spitting something about young upstarts thinking they ruled the world. Hebbings would say something that on the face of it was trying to calm him down, but really added fuel to the fire. Blanderley would—

"You've sure put the cat among the pigeons, haven't you, Leith? Hah! The looks on their faces!"

Peony went still. If her cat-face could frown, she would have frowned. Blanderley sounded genuinely amused.

"Where's that bottle? Here. You deserve a drink after that." Glass clinked and bubbles popped as someone poured champagne for Mordecai.

What is happening?

She'd expected the board to be irate about Mordecai's trick. Not celebrating it.

Is this what he'd planned? Peony's blood ran cold as she tried to make sense of what was going on. Beneath his shirt, Mordecai was stiff. He radiated displeasure—but that was his default, wasn't it? It didn't mean he wasn't celebrating with the rest of them. He was probably just being judgy about the venue still.

He let out a long, slow breath. Perfectly controlled as usual. Her own breath caught in her throat. "I must admit, I was expecting a little more pushback."

"You think we want to hold on to that old pile of junk?" Someone laughed. Peony curled up tighter, wishing she could turn off her ears. "You're doing us a favor, taking it off our hands. Hell, can I interest you in the shithouse block of apartments downtown?"

"Hell of a trick to play." Hebbings' raspy voice was rich with admiration. *I'm going to be sick,* Peony thought. "Blanders is right. You know, we've got our reputations to think of—can't go around throwing people out of their houses when you're running for council. You, though . . . no interest in politics, eh, Leith?"

"None whatsoever." She could have chipped shards off Mordecai's voice and used it as a murder weapon. But he wasn't all cold. Her cat tapped curiously at the icy shield around his mind and found a crack.

Rage boiled through, red-hot and fierce, before he hissed in a breath and locked himself away again.

Peony trembled.

"Well, if you want to take this other shithole off my hands, talk to my secretary . . ."

The conversation rolled over her, wave after wave breaking down everything she'd thought she had known. None of them had cared about the Hypatia. It had been a stone around their necks—a money sink, a waste of resources, more trouble than it was worth even to get permission to knock it down and get some value out of the site.

A waste of resources? None of you even spent anything on the building until it was literally falling down and I knocked on your doors begging for maintenance! The tiny spark of anger barely pushed back the tide, but it was enough that she suddenly felt she could breathe again. *I had to quote chapter and verse of local laws to get the elevator fixed! The stairs were a firetrap for years before I waved enough hazard reports in front of your noses that you had to do something about it!*

How had she never connected the dots before now? She had thought the board were absent-minded. A pack of old fuddy-duddies, but essentially all right. That was why she needed to put together full-blown proposals right down to the 'press this button to call an electrician to fix this' details whenever something went wrong.

But they weren't absent-minded.

They just didn't care.

Mordecai pulled an envelope from his other pocket. The sound of shuffling paper joined the clinking of glasses. They were signing something. Signing the rest of the building over to him?

So he could destroy it.

It shouldn't matter to her. It *couldn't* matter to her. The Hypatia wasn't important. It was just her backstory. Something she'd had to fill in time before her life began properly.

"Your new manager won't be joining us, Arthur?"

"God, I hope not. Last thing we need, her crying about her precious books. You know she still hasn't shut up about the goddamn hot water turning off last winter?"

Berwick chuckled. It was a nasty sound. "If it's not one thing with that woman, it's another."

"There's your silver lining, Arthur. No more whingy little—"

"I take it you're talking about Miss Fisher?" Mordecai was stiff as a statue. Tucked against his side, Peony could feel him trembling slightly, as though he was coiled tight with power that might explode at any second. *You brought me here for a reason, Miss Fisher. Is there anything you'd like me to say to them?*

His telepathic voice rolled through her, underscored by menace. Was she feeling his emotions, as well as hearing his words? None of her family ever mentioned that. It was so . . . intimate. Horribly intimate.

And there, beneath the promise of violence, something dark and scaled that blotted out the stars . . .

Peony's cat pricked up its ears at that, but the rest of her was too hollowed-out to pay attention. *No. I just want to leave.*

Mordecai stood. She tucked herself into an even tighter ball as he said something to the others. Then he was walking—through the tempest of scents that filled the club, past thumping bass that rattled through her tiny bones.

Out into the cold night air.

What now?

She couldn't think about what they'd said about her. It hurt too much. But the building—that hurt too, even though it shouldn't.

Blanderley and the others had hung on to the building like she hung on to old pencil-stubs. Not because they were useful, or she actually wanted them, but because there was always something more important taking up her attention. They hadn't even cared enough about the Hypatia to bother getting rid of it.

But Mordecai does. Why? Why did he care so much about the Hypatia that he'd gone to all this effort to destroy it?

6

Mordecai

Peony was too quiet.

You should have killed them. His dragon saw things very simply.

Just for once, he would have liked to see things simply, too.

He ground his teeth as his breath plumed out into the frosty air like an echo of the firestorm his dragon wanted to pour over the men he'd left toasting their good luck in the club.

If Peony had asked him to, he would have. Damn the consequences. The rage that had built inside him as he realized he'd been duped would have been so easy to let out. If she'd been angry, if she'd wanted her own white-hot revenge, he would have given it to her.

But she hadn't been angry. She was so quiet and so still that only the warm weight in his pocket reassured him she was still there.

Miss Fisher—

Don't. She could not have made it more painfully clear that she didn't want his help.

And what sort of help could you offer her? What good are you? You can't even get your own revenge right. Your life's work, and for what? They're happy. You didn't destroy them. You helped them.

Might as well have shined their shoes for them on your way out.

For one brief moment, he had thought that was why Peony had wanted to come to the meeting: to see his carefully laid plans come to nothing. He had imagined her conspiring with the others to humiliate him.

But the confusion and misery pouring from her mind set him right. And the way they'd talked about her . . .

Miss Fisher, he tried again. **Peony. Say something to me.**

I'd like to go home. Her voice was a tiny, frail thing. He wanted to take her in his hands and comfort her. **No, wait. I can't go there now. Not—**

Not when the Hypatia would echo with the cruel words of her boss and his friends.

He flexed his hand before he did something stupid like touch her.

Not the Hypatia, he said, and the relief that flooded into his mind from hers hurt. **I'll take you to my house.**

She didn't speak on the drive or during the excruciating elevator journey to his penthouse. Mordecai glared at his reflection in the elevator's mirrored walls and decided it was a good thing she couldn't see him like this. The doorman hadn't batted an eyelid when he'd walked in. The man deserved a raise; Mordecai looked like he was ready to murder someone.

Of course he didn't bat an eyelid. He's used to seeing you like this. Everyone is. But his mate?

I'm meant to be gentle for her. A lover. Not . . . this.

Even a human would be able to see the dragon in him like this. The doorman was probably going to have nightmares about burning villages.

He took one last look at his thunderous expression and bit back a sigh.

As though she doesn't already know who I am. Smiling and acting pleasant wouldn't save him now.

Still, he tried to wrestle back control over his face as he stalked to his apartment. By the time he was standing in his living space—his sanctuary, as he'd always thought of it—he at least no longer looked a hair's breadth from burning the entire city to the ground.

Peony was still silent in his pocket. He paused. "We're here."

Oh. She tentatively stuck her head out the top of his pocket.

He froze, suddenly unmoored in his own body. Knowing she was there was one thing, but seeing her ears twitch as she looked around the room sent him so far off his bearings it was either freeze or collapse.

She trusted me to hold her. To take her to where she wanted to go, while she was stuck in this tiny form. Nobody had ever trusted him like that before. *Every time I try to pull away, she comes one step closer to me.*

She looked around. He waited, silent, one arm held out oddly from his side because he suddenly didn't know what to do with it.

His apartment had everything money could buy. The finest materials and craftsmanship, every last detail perfectly designed to separate his sanctuary from the rest of the world. Elegant, understated furniture, the most minimal decoration his dragon would let him get away with, and the best atmospheric management system he'd been able to get his hands on.

Noticing the small details calmed him down. The moment he'd entered, the lights had adjusted to compensate for the ambient light elsewhere in the building, and the air filtration system had whirred into action to draw away the smells of the outside world he'd brought in with him. He wasn't sure what the automation would do to accommodate Peony in her cat form; he'd never had an animal here before.

Not even me, his dragon whispered.

You wouldn't fit. And— No. He wouldn't let himself think it.

But sometimes his dragon was one of the things he wanted to leave outside.

When Peony transformed back into her human form, the system would adjust to take account of her . . . of her . . .

Of her naked human body.

His mind whited out. All his thoughts were packed with snow, and he was buried in them, muffled and blinded.

Mordecai?

Had he done something to betray what was going through his mind? Made some sort of noise?

Holding himself stiff to keep his breath from shaking, Mordecai stared down at her. She blinked up at him. "Do you need my help getting out?" *Oh, well done. That didn't sound murderous. Just icily dismissive.*

No, I . . . I don't think so? She gathered herself up, a ball of fluff and muscles coiled like springs, and leapt.

She landed on all fours on the arm of the sofa. Her back

legs skidded and she dug her claws in, leaving tiny rents in the leather. Regret lanced against his mind.

Sorry! I didn't mean to—

He was about to tell her not to concern herself about it, when she turned her head back and forth, her tail lashing.

What's wrong with this place?

"Excuse me?"

It doesn't smell like anything.

Mordecai frowned. "I would have thought you'd consider that a good thing, considering how you almost lost control at Inferno."

I didn't almost lose control because of— Ugh. Really, though. It smells like NOTHING. She sounded affronted. Her nostrils twitched as she picked her way onto the back of the sofa, sniffing determinedly. Eventually her shining green eyes found him again. *I can't even smell YOU anymore!*

"Is that a good thing or a bad thing?"

I haven't decided yet!

They stared at each other. Mordecai's brain was still snow-muffled, which was the only excuse he had for what he said next.

"We should talk about what happened at Inferno."

Peony-the-cat shuddered. *No. We should never talk about it again.* Her private thoughts flew in an aura around her telepathic speech: *I'm too humiliated. How can I look any of them in the face again? I should have known . . .*

What am I meant to do now?

"This will be easier if we're both in human form." Mordecai

cleared his throat. "I'll give you some space. If you let me know your clothing size, I can have something brought in."

Brought in? How often do you have to clothe naked women in your apartment?

"You're the first woman I've ever brought here."

Gold-flecked green eyes searched his. *I believe you.*

"I wouldn't lie about—"

Because I don't think you actually live here. It smells too dead for that.

He stilled. "Dead?"

It's so . . . nothing. She moved her paws uneasily. *It's like nothing exists here. A void.*

Mordecai worked his jaw until he could trust himself to speak. "You can shift here or in the bedroom. The bathroom," he corrected himself as Peony let out a squeak. "You said it can take you a while to shift, so take all the time you need. I have staff on call who can purchase you anything you need."

What, like . . . a personal shopper? You don't need to buy me anything.

"You'd prefer to wear something of mine?"

Her tiny furry head snapped around. *What?*

"When you shift, you'll be naked," he said, slowly, scarcely able to believe he needed to say the words out loud.

You didn't, his dragon reminded him. *You could have spoken to her telepathically.*

Yes. Correct. He could have brushed the edges of her mind with his, his attention shivering down the connection between them like a plucked string, and said the word *naked* directly into her brain.

Oh. Right. Yes. I . . . I didn't think of that. Cats could not blush. But Peony's psychic voice had a very warm, pink feeling to it. *But first, can you take me to a mirror?*

His first instinct was to pick her up, protecting her tiny form within the safety of his hands, and carry her.

He quashed the impulse. *There is no way she would appreciate me manhandling her,* he told his dragon when it argued with him. *And the idea that she would find me to be a source of safety . . .*

He directed her to the en suite, somehow managing not to think about the fact they were passing through his bedroom. If she had been in human form— No. She'd made it clear she preferred to be in cat form around him, probably for that very reason.

The matebond was meant to be powerful, representing a strong physical and emotional connection between two people. *How much easier to ignore an unwanted attraction when you have needle-like teeth and claws and a whole world of sensory overload to block out your despised mate?*

He kept his thoughts well hidden. For a change, Peony was doing the same. She jumped onto the vanity and stared at herself in the mirror for a long minute, and all he felt from her was a tremor of . . . something.

He frowned.

Then—

This can't be happening. This can't be right. Her voice was hushed. She was trying to hide it.

Mordecai ignored a tic in his cheek. If she was trying to hide her thoughts, the polite thing to do would be to pretend he didn't hear them.

This rapidly became more difficult.

Peony's thoughts quick-fired through his brain, each one pricking like a tiny knife, too fast for him to follow. What was she reacting to?

Her cat form was ridiculously cute. Its fur was long and soft and the color of butterscotch, with white socks. Its eyes were huge, luminous green with flashes of gold that reminded him of the same flashes in her human eyes, although the base color was different. Brown in her human form, green in her cat form. When it meowed—which he was certain must have been accidental on her part—it was tiny and high-pitched and like something off a cartoon.

Fate must have been drunk when it paired the two of them: his brute of a dragon and this tiny, adorable creature. It was a cosmic joke.

This is what I put my life on hold for? Peony's voice was a horrified whisper.

Ice trickled down Mordecai's spine. Polite be damned.

"Regardless of the circumstances, you are my mate, and I am—" Something in his chest twisted painfully. "I am yours. We need to accept that."

How am I meant to accept it? Peony-the-cat's fur stood on end, her tail as stiff and fluffed-up as a wire brush, but it was her human face that burst into his memory. The way she had swallowed back her anger and disappointment back at the bookstore. He'd wanted to see her bare her claws then.

I should have been more careful what I wished for.

Peony's tail lashed. She sprang from the vanity and dashed back into his bedroom. *I don't care if it is fate! This can't be what's meant to be. What I'm meant to be. A person's mate is meant to be their perfect companion, someone who'll complement them and strengthen them, not some useless little—*

"Not me?" His voice was pure ice. It left his lips numb.

Peony-the-cat turned her luminous green eyes on him.

He realized, too late, that the expression in Peony-the-cat's eyes wasn't hatred. It was desperation. And the hurt in his chest wasn't only his own.

His mate was as profligate with her emotions as she was her thoughts, and he'd made the classic negotiating mistake of focusing on his opponent's words, not the feelings they hid.

You're also thinking of her as your opponent, his dragon whispered. He winced.

But it was too late. She hadn't seen desperation in his eyes; she'd seen ice and heartlessness. Her ears flicked back. She jumped up onto the bed, the better to glare at him.

You left, she accused him. *You saw me, and you must have known I was your mate then, and you stood up there and took everything away from me and then you LEFT.*

Her voice was a snarl in his head. The smell of rust and ashes filled his nose. *No, don't,* his dragon whispered urgently, but the words were already snapping from his frozen lips.

"Left what? You saw me. You felt what I did. Why would I stay when you clearly didn't want to acknowledge the connection between us?"

I didn't know!

Her psychic shout was so loud, it took him a second to piece out what she had actually said. He frowned. "What do you mean, you didn't know?"

She edged backwards, discomfort radiating from every hair on her body. *I didn't know. Okay? I couldn't tell you were my mate until I kissed you.*

"How is that possible?" He would have assumed she was lying, except she was so obviously unhappy that she'd revealed it. "All shifters recognize their mates on sight."

I wasn't a shifter then.

He stared at her cat form.

She tried to roll her eyes and almost fell off the side of the bed. *Yes, yes, okay, I know how it sounds. But I wasn't. My family are shifters, but not until we meet our mates. I don't know why it works that way for us, so don't ask me.*

"You've never shifted before today?" That explained why she hadn't been able to transform back into her human body. And— "Telepathy must be new to you, as well."

She sunk down low, a tiny cringing loaf. *Yeah. Explains a lot, doesn't it?*

"Your actions do seem a lot less mad, in hindsight." He sat down beside her.

That's nice of you to say, but I think we both know it's a lie. She sighed. It washed through his mind, and the fist-like knot in his chest loosened. *I've never . . . I don't . . .*

Her thoughts tumbled over one another. He waited for her to straighten them out. Her frustration made sense, now.

Her first shift. What had his first time been like?

Dark, his dragon said. *Cold.*

He shivered.

"It must have been hard, knowing you were a cat shifter but not being able to access that side of yourself," he said to fill the silence.

She flicked her whiskers at him. **I didn't know I was a cat shifter.**

"Did no one in your family—?" He stopped himself. If nobody in her family had found their mates, of course they wouldn't know they were cat shifters. But then how would they have known they were shifters at all? Was it a family legend? That would explain her frenzied reaction. If she had no point of reference for what it was like to shift, the sudden explosion of psychic abilities, no wonder she had found it difficult.

Shifter type isn't inherited in my family. It's random. No, not random, it's . . . The fur over her shoulders twitched. **It's a reflection of who we really are. Which means none of us really know our true inner selves until we meet our mate and shift for the first time. I always hoped . . . but that doesn't matter now.** She drew a ragged breath. The force of it in his mind shook him. **I spent my whole life waiting to find out who I am, and this is it. I'm tiny and cute and adorable and helpless.**

This has nothing to do with me after all. The relief was immediate and immediately followed by a rush of guilt. His mate was hurting, her whole understanding of her own nature turned on its head, and his first reaction was relief that he wasn't the target of her anguish?

"Your inner animal doesn't change who you are. If your cat is a reflection of your soul, then that must be who you've been your whole life already." Like he was a dragon. A creature of fire and vengeance and destruction.

Peony's laughter echoed hollowly along the connection that bound him to her. *Yeah. I guess this is who I have been. My whole life.*

She did not sound reassured.

"You should shift back. Some distance from your animal form might help." He almost reached for her, but stopped himself. "I was impatient with you before. I apologize."

She stared at him, her green eyes wide. *You APOLOGIZE?*

"For thinking you rejected me first. And for assuming you were remaining in this form to make things difficult."

You admit you rejected me, then. She looked away.

"I shouldn't have left."

Peony-the-cat didn't move. She kept her gaze averted. Even her ears didn't twitch. But her attention flowed towards him, bright and intense. He stilled. His dragon spread its wings uncertainly. It had always been the apex predator in any encounter. Other shifters, the few times he met them, barely dared to look him in the eyes.

And now, without even looking at him, his mate pried into his mind and stripped him bare.

Her attention burned the shadows from his mind. If she looked, she would see all of him. His dragon. His soul. Her psychic gaze would pierce the walls he kept things behind that even he didn't want to see.

But she stopped before she looked that far. She kept to the edges, then drew back. *You're telling the truth,* she said, shock echoing down their connection before she pulled away. There was a sensation of a door being closed, and he realized he'd been so stunned by having a spotlight on his mind that he'd never considered the openness might go both ways. *You really wouldn't have left?*

"I never gave any thought to the possibility I might find my mate," he admitted. "You say you've been waiting for your inner animal to give your life meaning. My life was laid out for me the moment mine emerged. And it has not been a life that had room for anything else in it."

He couldn't explain why he was so reluctant to reveal the nature of his inner animal.

Your brutish dragon, the dragon in question hissed at him.

Yes. Maybe that was the reason.

Her gold-flecked green eyes took in the room. Pale furnishings, cool lighting, featureless walls, and colorless bed linens.

As lifeless as the rest of my apartment. Which was an unpleasant thought. And that was strange: before now, he'd been quietly proud of his stripped-back living quarters. They provided no distraction from the important part of his life.

By contrast, Peony's cramped apartment had been full of life. Books and art and clothing, all the evidence of the life she claimed she was waiting to start. He grimaced.

She flicked an ear at him. *What are you thinking?*

"You can't tell?"

Seriously? I know I'm an open book right now, but you're not.

He raised one eyebrow. Inside him, his dragon attempted to do the same. *Strange words from a woman who just stripped away all my defenses.*

Not all, his dragon reminded him. *You haven't let her see me, yet. Or the walls. Or what's behind them. You don't even let yourself see what's behind them.*

He cleared his throat. "Do you want to attempt to shift back into human form?"

THAT'S what you were scowling about? She hesitated. **Yes. But like I completely failed to tell you earlier, I have no idea how.**

"Let me try to help with that."

She shot him a suspicious look.

And she's justified in doing so, he thought wryly. *She must have caught on to how I keep avoiding her questions by now.*

All right. I'd appreciate that. She rubbed her face with one white-socked paw, then added in an undertone he wasn't meant to hear, **Better than calling my folks and explaining it all to them.**

He could understand that. There were few things in life he would dread more than having to go to his grandmother for advice.

Which brought to mind further complications. Christmas was two days away; his grandmother would expect his presence at Christmas dinner, and a report on his life's work.

I'll save you that, at least, he promised his mate silently.

7.

PEONY

Mordecai was being nice.

She was appalled.

Hating him had been so easy. It had almost felt good, in a sick, twisted way, when he left Club Inferno without calling out the board on their comments about her. If her heart had to be cut out, he might as well stomp on it too. If there was no hope, then she could wallow in self-pity endlessly, as though she were a teenager again.

And then he'd brought her home and it had become horribly, awkwardly clear he'd made his excuses at the club in order to spare her the pain of listening to further insults, and he'd listened to her hiss and spit about him with all the anger she could no longer hide now that she was a shifter, and he had been *nice*.

He'd offered to buy her clothes. He wanted to help her.

His words echoed in her mind. *I wouldn't have left.*

Maybe there was still hope that this wasn't a tragedy after all.

Why was that a more terrifying thought than the idea that she was doomed?

She was still perched on his bed, the fact of which she'd become horribly aware the moment he said the word *naked*. Which was another appalling thought. She was a grown woman. She knew how shifters worked. How the matebond worked. The thought of being naked in front of her mate shouldn't make her want to squeal and roll into a ball like an embarrassed teenager.

How do I shift back, then?

A pause. "You want to try it here?" Unsaid: here in my bedroom? On my bed?

She wasn't *actually* reading his mind. That one moment of absolute, hair-raising connection as her cat raced into his mind to find out if he was lying to her was bad enough.

She didn't need telepathy to know that was what he meant. And once he'd said it—or not said it, whatever—there was no way she was going to move.

I can't imagine anything less erotic than this catalogue-photo bedroom, anyway. Even the water glass on the bedside table looked as though, if you touched it, alarms would go off and a store employee would tell you off for touching the display.

Here's as good as anywhere, she said.

Mordecai frowned. How much of what she'd just thought about his bedroom had he heard?

"More than I expect you intended me to," he muttered. His eyes creased at the corners. Was that a smile? Was he *smiling*?

First he's nice, now he's smiling at me? she thought, as quietly as she could.

His spine straightened, almost imperceptibly. He stood up and moved to the armchair in front of the window. She felt a surge of ridiculous irritation. From the awkward way he planted himself in the chair, it was the first time he'd ever sat in it.

Why have a flash apartment like this if you're going to treat it like you don't even live there?

"I first shifted when I was thirteen," he said. "My grandmother had been expecting me to shift since my eleventh birthday, which was when my father first shifted. It would have caused . . . problems . . . for my first shift to occur in public, so she would take me down to the basement of our building and encourage me to search for my inner animal. Perhaps the same would work in reverse. If you look inside yourself and seek out your human self."

Her stomach sank. Seek out her human self? She barely knew who that was, now. *Someone best represented by a tiny, helpless fluffball.*

But—

Wait. You hung out in a basement, waiting for your inner animal to appear? From when you were eleven until when you were thirteen?

"Not permanently. She let me out for fresh air on the weekends," he joked dryly. She hoped it was a joke. "As I said, the consequences if I'd shifted uncontrolled in front of a non-shifter would have been disastrous."

He didn't need to explain why. No matter what his inner animal was, no shifter wanted to reveal the existence of magic to all and sundry. The world was complicated enough as it was.

Still.

Two years. When he was just a kid.

Maybe waiting for your inner animal to show up until you were a grown-up and sucked face with the right person wasn't so uniquely terrible, after all.

What sorts of things did you focus on, trying to find your inner animal?

"Sensory experiences. At least, what I assumed the sensory experiences of my . . . of it would be."

She caught the slight hesitation, and her eyes narrowed. *He's hiding what his inner animal is. Why? The same reason he keeps avoiding all my questions? Maybe it's something really embarrassing. Like a squid. Or a toad. Or—*

Wait. What if he actually is a frog?

The thought cheered her more than it should have. Maybe they were a good match, after all.

I hope he didn't hear that.

She told herself sternly to focus. Sensory experiences. The way she experienced the world as a cat was so vivid—*The smells! The sounds!*—but it wasn't *all* an improvement on her human senses.

Her cat didn't have great near vision. It didn't have opposable thumbs. It was good at jumping, but it had to be because it was so damned short. She'd had to jump up on this bed just so she wasn't yowling at Mordecai from a million miles below him.

The bed . . .

There were other things her cat didn't have, either. All the treacherous soft, hot feelings she hadn't been able to ignore before she shifted. They were still there, waiting, but they weren't as utterly distracting as they had been.

Where were they waiting?

Somewhere deep inside her. She closed her eyes.

And was immediately distracted.

A basement? Really? Someone as rich as him couldn't afford a private warehouse or something to hang out in waiting to shift? She opened her eyes again. Mordecai's gaze was distant.

Is he talking to his . . . whatever he is? Her stomach dropped. She'd imagined lots of things about what meeting her mate would be like, but not how she'd have so little control over her telepathy. She was so exposed, and he was so icily controlled.

There had been a moment before when she'd almost felt as though she'd broken through his shell. She'd been so surprised by his pronouncement that he shouldn't have left her that she chased his thoughts back to their hiding-place. And as soon as she'd gone down that road, she'd realized what it was. The matebond. A literal—well, a magical—bond. Like a ribbon.

Or a chain.

Her heart skittered at the memory.

She'd been outside her own mind. She hadn't known what it was like to be *inside* her own mind until then. Being in Mordecai's mind had felt wrong, and dangerous, but a delirious sort of dangerous, like if she'd just reached further then something wonderful would have happened.

So of course she'd jumped back as quickly as she could.

Could I do it again? Would she want to? Yes, her cat said at once. It flexed its claws. *We should go back and find out MORE.*

Which was technically a horrible thing to consider—breaking and entering somebody's *mind*—but also kind of tempting. No, it wasn't the idea of sneaking into his mind that attracted her (her cat disagreed strenuously).

It was the idea of Mordecai Leith, he of the unscalable cheekbones, losing control enough to let her hear his inner thoughts. *Oh YES*, her cat said, changing its mind at once. Could she make him do that? She imagined his frosty calm cracking. What would it be like?

What would it HAVE been like, if I hadn't shifted when he kissed me? He'd tried to control himself. It had lasted all of a second. She remembered his mouth opening beneath hers. His hunger for her. There hadn't been anything icy about it.

Could I do it again?

"Miss— Peony?"

She shook herself. *Sorry? Yes?*

"This is clearly not working." Mordecai ran his long fingers through his hair and sat back broodily. Outlined by the lights of the city below, he looked like an evil king about to pass judgement. "We'll have to consider other methods."

Other methods like what? Drinking from the wrong side of a cup? Scaring me human again?

"This is magic, not the hiccups."

Seeing him sitting so calmly on the chair was . . . annoying. *I'd like to see him sprawling on it.*

The thought arrived fast and vicious, like a cat-scratch, and filled Peony's mind. Mordecai lying on his back, all his fastidious calm lost. His shirt—also lost. His lips parted. His eyes black-flooded with lust, but good luck to him if he thought he was going to be able to do anything about it, because this was *her*—

"Are you listening to me?"

Y-yes? Oh sweet baby Santa. I really, really hope he didn't catch any of that.

He glared at her suspiciously. "Catch any of what?"

Nothing?

He sighed, exasperated. "I'm sure you want to get this over with as much as I do. You mentioned your family. If they've been through the same experience as you, they might be able to offer you advice—"

I thought you said this was magic, not hiccups? Why are you trying to scare me into shifting? She meowed. *Let me just try one more thing.*

"Which is?"

Had she ever thought he was nice? She must have been dreaming. He was back to full Evil Count mode, sitting in that damned chair with his eyes like chips of black diamonds.

A development of your first theory. Instead of thinking animal thoughts, I'm going to try thinking human thoughts.

"Human thoughts."

You know the sort. Taxes. Laundry. Mordecai lying flat on his back, his dark hair fanned out around his head in stark contrast to the boring white sheets.

"Those are the things you consider essentially human?" A sliver of life peeked through his icy mask. *Aha.*

Some of them. I thought it would be too awkward to bring up the other ones. Mordecai, hot and bothered, pinned beneath her thighs, straining as he ground his hips against—

The Mordecai sitting opposite her frowned. "What are you thinking about?"

Human things.

He leaned forward, his gaze suspicious. "Taxes."

Unemployment. Maybe that's why I'm staying a cat. Don't need to pay the rent if I can find some nice family to take in a poor sad kitty at Christmas.

"You—" He cut himself off. His eyes narrowed. "You're baiting me."

You don't think it's a good idea?

If he hadn't been so iceberg-chill, she expected he would have ground his teeth. As it was, his eyes flashed extremely obligingly. "I thought we established that I regretted walking away from you."

Her heart fluttered. He was so *grumpy*. Would he bring that resentment into the bedroom?

Why was the thought of that so goddamn hot?

Still, I'm out an apartment. And a job. Thanks to you, my fated soulmate. She waited a beat. *You have to admit it's not ideal. Given the circumstances.*

The lines around his mouth deepened. "I agree," he said, every word a chip of the deep cold between the stars. "The circumstances are not ideal for romance."

The seconds stretched out. And then—she couldn't help it.

She burst out laughing.

He stared at her, looking suddenly off-balance and, oh god, the uncertainty in his eyes. The surprise. *That* was what she wanted. If she could only push him a little further—

Then what? She would need to be human to do any of the things that immediately sprang to mind. To shove him back on the butter-soft leather. To make his eyes widen with surprise. To make him make noises. Noises like the groan he'd made when she'd pressed her lips against his, the groan that was going to live rent-free in her head for the rest of her life, taunting her. She would need—

Whoosh.

8

Mordecai

The air around cat-Peony shivered.

It happened too quickly for him to look away. One minute he was leaning forward, elbows on his knees as he glared suspiciously at a tiny ball of fluff. He was sure she was up to something.

The next, a naked woman was perched on the edge of his bed.

He leapt to his feet. Shocked gold-brown eyes met his. Color brightened her already warm-toned cheeks. Her lips were lush and open. The rest of her—

With great effort, he averted his gaze and shrugged off his suit jacket. She took it from his outstretched hand. Her fingers brushed his. He pulled away swiftly as though that one touch might scald him.

His heartbeat filled his throat. All his senses were on high alert. He pushed them back. It wasn't right. He'd only seen her for a single stolen second. His mind, his heart, shouldn't already be so full of the sight of her. The scent. The rush of heat that had seared through his blood as she stared at him, and the accompanying hardness that meant he absolutely could not turn back to her quite yet.

She was spectacular.

I am so fucked.

Now turn around and enjoy how she looks wearing your gift, his dragon suggested. He gritted his teeth. *I understand now why she didn't want you to buy her new clothes. This is much better!*

It was so much worse. And his dragon was right: he would enjoy looking at her far too much.

Movement behind him. A soft footstep. Another. He tensed. Was she . . .?

"This is awkward, isn't it?" Her breath tickled his ear.

"Yes."

And the circumstances, as they had both so thoroughly agreed, were not ideal. She seemed like a sensible person. He waited for the soft shush of fabric over softer skin to tell him it was safe to turn around.

It never came.

"Am I making you uncomfortable?"

He'd thought having her voice in his head was intimate. It was nothing compared to having her hot breath on his neck. The gentle catch in her words that felt like a lure deliberately cast to reel him in.

"Yes."

"Do you want me to stop?"

She wasn't even touching him. She was just there—right behind him, so close that if he breathed too deeply he might brush up against her. Naked. Teasing.

His.

"Are you sure?" His own voice was a dry husk.

"I wouldn't have started if I wasn't sure."

He could hear her smile. It lilted the edges of her words and made him feel as though his feet had left the ground.

How is this happening? He replayed the last several minutes of their conversation. The whole painful half-dozen hours since they'd met. None of it added up.

Except the most obvious, impossible equation: that she was his mate and he was hers and she wanted him as much as he wanted her. And she hadn't locked herself inside her animal form to stay away from him, after all.

He wet his lips. "You shouldn't feel obligated to—"

"Of all the— No. I don't feel obligated to do *anything* in regards to you. The circumstances took care of that." She made an amused *huff*, and he couldn't imagine how she was managing to find the situation amusing.

"That's good." His teeth clacked shut.

Neither of them moved. Peony didn't retreat, but she didn't get closer, either. Didn't touch him. The brush of her breath on his neck was driving him mad.

He tensed his jaw. "If you've changed your mind, you can leave."

"I'm still waiting for you to answer my question."

"What?" He spun around, eyebrows furrowing. God almighty, she was right there. Naked and soft and more glorious than anything in his life had any right to be.

Her eyes danced. Was the gold in them stronger than it had been when he first saw her?

He stared, speechless, and her smile widened.

"I really thought it would be more difficult than this," she said, a shade ruefully, and brushed his hair back off his forehead with one delicate finger. Fire blazed across his skin where she touched him.

"What would be more difficult?" There was no trace of fire in his voice. It was as though the turmoil raging in his veins made his outward self even frostier. He sounded like the world's worst prig.

Worse. It sounded as though he was rejecting her. As though he was standing here, in the spun-gold spotlight of her eyes, her warm bare body only inches from his, and wasn't affected.

She'll hate me for this.

He waited for the light to go out of her eyes.

Instead, her smile widened, cat-like.

"You can't tell?" Her eyes widened. "You can't hear me thinking about it?"

He shook his head wordlessly. The connection between them was humming, but it was . . . muted. Not the roar of input it had been when she was in cat form.

"Hmm." Her eyebrows twitched. Momentarily, her gaze turned inwards. He watched entranced as she seemed to focus intently on something beyond his reach. "Maybe my telepathy is less strong in human form?"

"Perhaps you have more control over it when you're in a shape that's more familiar to you."

"Shouldn't it feel stranger to have new powers in a familiar body, than the body and the powers both being new? Or it could be that since I have no other way of communicating in cat form, my psychic powers compensate. Or—" Her eyes narrowed. "Excuse me."

"Yes?"

"I'm trying to get a straight answer out of you, not get distracted into a discussion about the hows and whys of telepathy."

"Is that so?"

"Yes!"

"You've asked me several questions. Which one did you want me to answer?"

This had to be a dream. If it was real life, he would have been able to take control of the conversation as he normally did. If it was real life, Peony would have grown as frustrated by his constant conversational detours and eddies as he was. Why couldn't he tell her what he really wanted to say?

What do I want to say?

He didn't know. No. He knew, he just didn't know how to say it. He'd trained himself to lock target on his goals and pursue them with ruthless efficiency—he couldn't treat Peony that way.

But he didn't know how else to be.

So he kept picking up her suggestions and insinuations and tossing them aside. In a moment, she would give up and storm off, or—worse, so much worse it made his chest lock up—she would crumple in on herself. Like she had at the bookshop.

Instead, she tipped her head back. Cat-like green flashed in her gold-brown eyes, and her full lips twitched with mischief. "Good point. I should learn to be more specific. In no particular order, then: You confirmed that you can't hear all my thoughts right now, but you never answered whether you can tell what it is I thought would be more difficult about this situation."

She regarded him with a teasing patience that surely violated the Geneva Convention.

She was naked as sin in front of him, and she was asking him *questions*.

"In answer to that question," he forced out. "No. I can't tell."

Her lips quirked. "Next, and again in no particular order, do you want me to stop whatever it is that you claim you don't know I'm doing?"

He was the world's greatest idiot. He should kiss her. Hold her. Press her backwards onto the bed and do all the filthy things his mind was conjuring up.

But he couldn't move. The ice he'd spent years building around his heart paralyzed him.

"No," he choked out.

She moved closer, and his senses flooded. Her scent. The heat of her body.

"I think I'll skip the telepathy questions. They were more rhetorical, anyway." She stood on her tiptoes, her lips a whisper away from his. "Can you still not tell what I want?"

He had to say something. He was losing control of the situation, not like a runaway train but like a warm, slow-moving river buoying him up and floating him away.

You never had control of this situation in the first place, his dragon informed him. He thought he heard it laughing.

"Whatever it is, I imagine you'll begin by kissing me again."

Kill me now, his dragon groaned.

Peony laughed out loud. "Close," she said and dropped to

her knees.

His brain whited out. She was kneeling in front of him, her hand pressed against the seam of his pants. Pressed against him. Feeling just how hard he was.

The one part of me not frozen into paralysis. He wasn't sure whether he was grateful or embarrassed.

She ran her hand down his length, exploring every inch of him through the fabric of his trousers.

Grateful. Oh god.

She pulled him out, and his knees almost buckled. He needed to steady himself, but there was nothing to hold on to except her, and he couldn't—

Her hand, hot around his cock. The sight of her holding him, so close to her face, her lush lips, seared into his mind. And the expression in her eyes. Curious and excited and *calculating*, and somehow that made him even harder, the idea that she was looking at his cock like it was a puzzle she wanted to work out.

Her eyes flicked up to meet his, and he made a noise. He didn't even know what the noise was.

But Peony's gaze turned to pure fire. "I should tell you now that I don't have a whole lot of experience with this," she admitted, and he would have called her tone dry except for the teasing light in her eyes. "Mostly what I've read in books."

His hand clenched involuntarily on thin air. "That's not—"

She put her mouth on him.

His brain stopped functioning.

He didn't know what to do with himself. What was left of his brain was sending him urgent, fragmented messages. *Don't be too eager. Don't thrust into her mouth. For the love of god, don't grab hold of her head to steady yourself.*

But his body was drowning, overwhelmed by the wet heat of her mouth, the lap of her tongue on his shaft, the suction of her lips around him as she gave his length a curiously assessing look and took him deeper. The caressing current around him was heading for a waterfall, and there was nothing he could do to stop it.

"Peony—"

"Hmm?"

Oh god. She learned this from books?

"You can learn a lot from books." She lifted her gaze to meet his shocked eyes. Then, mouth full—oh fuck, fuck, *fuck*—added: **Wait. You didn't say that out loud, did you?**

He could reply telepathically. But if he did, it would all be over. The brush of her mind against his was bad enough; if he twined his thoughts with hers, he wouldn't be able to last. And he never wanted this to end.

She hummed laughter against his cock and withdrew. "Books can be very educational. I'm glad all my hours studying have turned out so useful."

He stared at her, utterly undone by this incredible, confusing woman who treated his body like a puzzle to solve. A puzzle she *wanted* to solve.

She smiled and ran her tongue long and slow down the bottom of his shaft. His whole body clenched.

He'd been desired before. It usually started when people found out about his money, and ended when they found out about his personality. But he'd never had anything like this. Like *her*. She was chasing his orgasm not to ingratiate herself with him but because figuring out what brought him to the edge gave her a sense of implacable satisfaction. A psychic purr that radiated from her like the rays of the sun.

He was about to come harder than ever before in his life, and his head was spinning at the thought that it was more about *her* than it was about him.

Why shouldn't it be? She's my mate. Everything I do should be about her.

He was so close. "Wait," he forced out, his hand flexing a half-inch from Peony's face. "Stop."

She stopped. Her gaze flicked from his face, to his hand, and back to his face. A silent question thrummed along the connection between them, and his knees almost gave way.

God, he wanted to touch her so much.

"Get on the bed," he rasped out. "I want to finish inside you."

"He speaks!" She rose, hands running hot and possessive over his shirt. "*You* get on the bed."

He could not think of any sensible rebuttal to that. He stumbled past her and, gathering the last strands of his dignity around him, sat.

She shoved him flat on his back and straddled him.

"Oh yes," she gasped, pinning him to the mattress like a nymph from some ancient myth—a creature of lust and magic and wonder, who might save him or might kill him. She was slick and hot against him, and he bucked his hips, thoughts disintegrating in the face of his mate's desire. "*This* is what I wanted. Exactly this."

He'd been wrong about her psychic powers being lessened in this form. Her emotions blazed like the stars. Joy. Giddy glee. And lust so fierce and hot it shocked the breath from him.

She lowered herself onto him with excruciating care. Her eyes never left his. Whatever she saw in his face made her purr with satisfaction. He could imagine her sharpening her claws on the sheets either side of his head. Instead she buried her hands in his hair and kissed him, the way he'd thought she would earlier, except now she tasted of him and he was inside her, lost in how hot and tight and wet she was as she eased herself down to his hilt and moved above him like an angel of sin.

"Go on," she whispered, drawing back enough to stare down into his eyes. *Let go.*

He came so hard he saw stars. Then her hands were on his shoulders, fingers digging in. The thought lurched through his mind—he should touch her, worship her body, make sure he was reciprocating the pleasure she was so joyously and insistently giving him—but his body wouldn't obey. Even as pleasure crashed through him, the paralysis held him in its grip.

Her body clamped tight as a fist, milking every last drop from him, and she cried out with a gasping moan.

She collapsed on top of him, sweaty and boneless in the wake of an orgasm that had torn through her like a storm. When she lifted her head at last, her gold-brown eyes seeking his, she looked dazed. "Better," she breathed. When he frowned, she laughed. "Exactly what I wanted. Even better than what I imagined."

It wasn't until much later that night, as she lay sleeping beside him and he lay stiffly awake, staring at the ceiling, that he could finally admit to himself why her words filled his stomach with ice.

She'd enjoyed herself. But *he* had had nothing to do with it. She'd taken pleasure in his body, and he would offer it to her as often as she wanted it—but that pleasure hadn't been a fair transaction. Not when he'd done nothing to bring her to her own climax.

He closed his eyes, and that was worse, without even the blank expanse of the ceiling to distract him from the ice filling his veins.

What if he couldn't? What if his mate could bring him and herself to such heights of pleasure that it left him undone—and he couldn't do the same for her?

9

PEONY

Was last night real? Did I really . . . yep. Yep, I did. And that.

And THAT.

All the things.

Holy crap. Who am I?

Peony woke up without a crick in her neck for the first time in years. She lifted her head and blinked.

Wow. I guess using a hot guy's chest as your pillow really is the most ergonomic choice.

Mordecai was still deeply asleep. His chest rose and fell in a slow, regular rhythm beneath her. His chest, muscular under the shirt that somehow she hadn't actually gotten around to tearing off him. His sculpted collarbones and the column of his neck heading up to his fierce, aristocratic profile.

Even in sleep his eyebrows were caught in a permanent scowl. It shouldn't have been attractive, but somehow it was the sexiest thing she'd ever seen.

Well. *Almost* the sexiest. It had a way to go to beat the sight of him stretched out beneath her, shirt rumpled, suit trousers open with his cock jutting out and his broken-glass eyes wide and shattered.

Her heartbeat sped up. Yes. That had been . . . wow.

And he was still lying under her. Vulnerable. Unprotected.

Her fingers twitched, but she pushed the instinct back. *I don't care how funny it would be to see him jump,* she told her inner cat. *I'm going to let him sleep.*

Because she needed all the time she could get to get her head straight.

Mordecai was her mate. Forget all her angst about her soul's true reflection being a tiny fluffy kitty for a moment—scorching hot, mega-asshole Mordecai was her mate.

Is he a mega-asshole, though? He'd been surprisingly kind to her once she'd told him the truth about it being her first shift. He was a bit of a prick, sure, but whatever animal lurked behind his eyes, it was powerful. So powerful that she suspected the reason he was keeping it hidden from her was to stop her freaking out more than she already had.

We could find out. Her cat crept forward, pinprick claws at the ready.

Nope. No, thank you. If Mordecai wanted to keep his inner animal a secret, she could wait until he was comfortable telling her.

It wasn't as though she had a leg to stand on when it came to keeping secrets from her mate, after all.

And the sex had been so good.

She closed her eyes and groaned. *So good.*

Am I really turning into the sort of person who can be won over by a single amazing orgasm?

Apparently so. Peony Fisher: tiny fluffy cat shifter,

emotionally sabotaged by her pussy.

Not the life she'd envisaged for herself, but . . .

"You're awake."

Her cat jerked up. Mordecai's breathing hadn't changed; had he been awake the whole time she was staring at him?

"Mm," she said, rolling off him. "Good morning."

He cracked open one dark eye and regarded her warily. *Is it?*

"Did you mean for me to hear that?"

". . . Yes." He rose slowly. "How do you feel?"

Achy. Delicious. Maybe ready for round two? "Um. Good?"

He narrowed his eyes. *Does he not believe me?* she wondered, amazed. *Did . . . Was he not here last night? Did he not see me have the most incredible orgasm of my life?*

"We should—" A muscle ticked in his jaw. He continued with barely a pause, but she got the strong suspicion that he had veered away from what he'd been planning to say. "It's Christmas Eve. What do you want to do?"

"Normally I'd head to work . . ." She swallowed and looked at the clock beside the bed. "I would have already gone to work."

And she didn't know how she felt about that.

No more bookstore.

No more Hypatia.

No more—

She took a deep breath. *That was the prologue of my life. Remember? It was a placeholder. It doesn't matter.*

Mordecai was watching her closely. "Peony?"

"Breakfast," she said firmly. "I'd like breakfast. And a shower.

And—" She grimaced. "I suppose I'd better take you up on your offer to get me some more clothes."

"I don't understand why you sound so resentful about that."

Because clothes shopping is the worst. Could he hear her think that? No, he couldn't hear her thoughts clearly when she was human. They'd established that last night.

"I hate online shopping," she said at last. "Even if clothes have measurements on them, they always fit weird, or the fabric isn't right, or they send the wrong thing anyway."

"I'll call my tailor."

"So I can stand around in my underwear while someone runs a measuring tape around me?" His eyes flashed, suddenly and gratifyingly possessive. "No, thank you. I'll risk buying off the mystery rack."

"Hmmph."

Wow. Did he just huff at me? The full strangeness of the situation hit her again. She was in bed with her mate. The next chapter of her life—the *first* chapter of her life—wasn't just about to start, it was here. She was living it.

Her chest twinged.

And she was a shifter. She had found her inner animal, and there it was, inside her, making the odd attempt to convince her to tickle her fingernails along Mordecai's ribs but otherwise apparently content to nap.

She was a new person. This was the rest of her life.

But . . .

"There is one other thing I'd like to do," she said. Mordecai's eyes pinned her. She resisted the urge to flex her claws. "The bookstore."

"Of course." He sounded calm, but he *felt* as though he was bracing himself.

"Christmas Eve is a big shopping day for us. I'm not . . . I'm not saying we should open the store. But a lot of our regular customers were expecting to pick up their orders today. In the name of tying up loose ends, I'd like to make sure they all get their books."

"That's all?"

"Yes." Of course it was. This was the rest of her life they were talking about. The bookstore was part of her prologue—but leaving things undone there wasn't a satisfactory ending.

That was the only reason.

She raised her chin. "It's the day before Christmas," she declared. "And I have a job to do."

Of course, the job had to wait on a few things. Like clothes. Her phone conversation with Mordecai's personal shopper Alessio ranked among the most embarrassing of her life. She was sure the poor guy almost fainted when she told him where she usually shopped. And then *she* almost fainted from embarrassment trying to explain why she couldn't turn on video or send a photo to give him an idea of what she looked like, because no way was she sending a photo of her bra-less, sleep-headed self, wrapped in one of Mordecai's robes, to some poor random guy.

Then there was breakfast.

Mordecai offered to make food, which was the biggest surprise of the morning so far. She'd imagined he would have a personal chef or ordered all his food in or just glared evilly at the kitchen counter until the universe got so scared it made food magically appear there. But no. Apparently, he cooked.

He headed to the kitchen; she headed straight for the shower. The en suite was less intimidatingly huge and glaring white than it had seemed in her cat form, but it was still as grimly bland as the rest of the apartment. Even the shower pressure was absolutely unexceptional.

What is the point of being so rich if you can't even scald yourself alive under a pressure hose?

Her hair was a mess, and she briefly regretted not asking Mordecai's shopper to pick her up some product. Mordecai's bathroom cabinet was stocked, but with the sort of expensive stuff that barely had labels. No way was she going to risk her curls with any of those.

She stood and rotated under the water until it became clear that showering wasn't going to help her thoughts become any clearer, then wrapped herself in one of Mordecai's robes—colorless, austere, possibly stolen from some sort of ascetic monastery that specialized in not-quite-soft-enough linen—and headed for the kitchen.

Mordecai's eyes went inky black when he saw her.

"Did you find everything you needed?" There was a rich burr beneath the polite question that made her shiver with delight.

"Yeah. Just waiting on the clothes, now."

"So I see." He made a vague gesture as though he meant to get back to what he was doing, but his eyes stayed fixed on her.

She rocked back on her heels, inordinately pleased. "Oh. Am I doing this wrong? You wanted me to wait for my clothes to arrive, not borrow one of your robes?" She slid the linen robe down over her shoulders.

Color lashed across Mordecai's face. For one moment, hunger filled his eyes. "If you do that, I have serious concerns about whether we'll ever make it through breakfast." His eyes flicked to the food he was preparing. "Perhaps that would be a good thing."

They both stared at the counter.

"Uh," Peony said after a minute. "What is this I'm looking at, here?"

"A nutritionally balanced meal."

Peony's cat woke up enough to sniff suspiciously at the packets next to the blender. *That isn't food,* it complained. *It's dirt.*

"Balanced between what?" she blurted out. "Blandness and boredom?"

"Precisely." His voice was dry. She looked at him, surprised, and found a spark of humor in his eyes. "I'm a busy man. I don't have time to worry about what I eat." He sighed. "But this isn't good enough for you."

"Oh, no, I can cope with a . . . a nutritionally balanced smoothie." She sucked in her lips. "This is all going to be a smoothie, right? We're not going to snort the protein powder straight off the counter?"

He made a frustrated noise. "Oat milk or almond?"

"Which would be more nutritionally efficient?" Her stomach growled, and she put her hand over it. "I'm not kidding. I'm *starving.* I will literally hoover that calorie-dust off the ground if you don't get it in a glass for me soon."

"That's not surprising. You barely ate yesterday, and you shifted for the first time. It takes a lot of energy." He looked away from her, and his mouth twisted. "I'll offer you something better next time."

She blinked. He sounded almost . . . ashamed?

Mordecai Leith? Evil necromancer, sexy asshole, destroyer of bookstores? Ashamed?

No. I must have got that wrong.

"As a matter of fact, I ate plenty yesterday. Mostly cheese and those tiny sausages on sticks." *And one massive saus— No. Stop. Not appropriate over breakfast.*

The smoothie he made was nutritionally dense and an efficient way to ingest calories. It took one minute to make, and two for them each to drain their glasses.

Afterwards, they both stared at the empty tumblers.

"Well," Peony said at last. "That was certainly food." Her eyelid twitched. "Okay, point taken. My cat would like to point out that it was only *potentially* food."

"I understand."

"It would like to lay an official complaint."

"Also very understandable."

"Frankly, Mr. Leith, I—"

"Call me Mordecai."

Their eyes met. Warmth kindled inside her. Oh, who was she kidding? She was already warm. The heat inside her barely needed a word from him to burn out of control. If he touched her . . .

. . . but he wouldn't do that, would he?

She frowned. Had Mordecai ever touched her first? She'd kissed him, then she'd gone down on him, then pushed him onto the bed—and obviously there'd been touching involved, but had he ever reached out to her?

No.

No, he hadn't.

Mordecai's phone dinged. He made a frustrated noise—one of his delightful arsenal of grumbles and huffs—and checked it. It was only as he dropped it into his pocket again that she realized that before he'd picked up his phone, he'd been staring at her.

He couldn't read her mind like this—she was almost certain of that. But what had he seen on her face?

He returned a minute later, arms laden with shopping bags. "Your clothes," he said.

Peony started. "There has to be some mistake. I didn't order that many things."

"I told Alessio to use his discretion."

Is 'discretion' code for 'go hog wild and buy up the whole store'? Peony stared. There were clothes from brands she hadn't even heard from. "I don't even know where to start. I told Alessio one pair of warm pants and a top from a place that I know the sizing works for me." And a bra and panties. For some reason, she could jump on Mordecai's cock like there was no tomorrow but not mention the word 'panties' in front of him.

Mordecai made an uncomfortable hmmph, then made himself scarce.

Okay, she thought. *What about this situation is making HIM uncomfortable, again? I'm the one who has to pick through a pile of clothes someone else bought for me when all I wanted was some fleecy leggings and a big sweater.*

Maybe that was it. Given how totally un-cosy his robe was, perhaps Mordecai was allergic to comfortable clothing.

She began to sort through the bags. Alessio had done a decent job, she had to admit. There *were* fleecy leggings and sweaters—expensive ones. And warm winter dresses and jackets—*multiple* jackets, as though quality winter coats just grew on trees—and boots. Boots in different colors. So that she could match them to the coats.

The whole sending-out-your-personal-peasant-to-buy-clothes was still weird, but . . . this was kind of cool, actually.

Then she found the lingerie bags.

Maybe this is why Mordecai left, she thought. *Hiding from my enormous, practical upholstery bras.*

Except her mate's on-call shopper had gone above and beyond in this department, too.

"Holy holly . . ." She held up a confection of lace and satin. "How does this even go on?"

Ask him to help you figure it out!

Peony bit her tongue. Although . . . maybe her cat had a point. She did need to work off that horrible breakfast somehow, and Mordecai . . .

She sighed and closed her eyes. *Mordecai.*

Even thinking his name sent a lick of excitement through her. She had never wanted anyone as much as she wanted him. The sex last night had been the best of her life. If spending the rest of her life with him meant more of that, then sign her up. Even if it meant the Hypatia—

A pang twisted in her chest. She shook herself. The Hypatia was part of her old life, not her new, mated life.

And once she tied off those loose ends today, she would be able to farewell it happily.

Right?

10

Mordecai

Keeping out of the way while Peony tried on her new clothing was the most painful thing Mordecai had ever done.

His dragon was no help. It kept helpfully suggesting that he go and make use of himself—holding bags, offering compliments, rending all her new clothing into tiny pieces so she couldn't wear it after all and they had to spend the day in bed together.

His cock twitched. God, he wanted . . .

. . . *her to be happy.*

And what she wanted, what would make her happy right now, was to spend the day running around doing errands for her work.

It had to be a trick.

He had spent a lifetime learning to see past people's words to what they actually meant, and his mate wanted the Hypatia. It obviously meant something to her. So if today was a way for her to line up the pieces and get ready to knock him down, he had to prepare.

To be knocked down again? his dragon suggested.

He shook his head impatiently. There had to be something she would want as much as the Hypatia, and he had to get it for her. Because the Hypatia wasn't an option.

Mordecai?

Heat rushed through him at Peony's hesitant question. "Yes?"

She poked her head around the door. "Good, that worked. Also, I'm ready to go, if you are."

"Yes." There were other words in his vocabulary, and he'd intended to say something about . . . he couldn't remember. Peony came into the room, wrapped in a snug woolen dress that held her as close as he wanted to, and anything approaching words disappeared from his mind.

He cleared his throat. Still nothing. Cleared it again. "You look lovely."

Warmth bloomed across her cheeks. "Thanks. Alessio did a great job."

Murder Alessio, his dragon suggested.

What? Why?

She likes the clothes he got her.

On our orders!

Nevertheless . . . His dragon sank back, grumbling possessively.

"The underwear, especially." Peony did an elaborate stretch-and-wiggle that shut down what was left of his higher brain function. "Honestly, I'm amazed. Even *I* don't do as good a job bra shopping for myself as this. It's like he knows my boobs better than I do."

Murder Alessio, Mordecai and his dragon thought in unison.

Then he caught the glint of mischief in his mate's eye. An answering smile crept across his face, long and slow and knife-sharp.

He was going to enjoy this game.

🦇 ⚅ 🦇

"Books." His voice gave nothing away. "People still give books for Christmas?"

"Of course they do!" Peony sounded outraged.

He hid a grin. They were back at the bookstore. Peony had looked at the *Closed* sign with an expression of such simmering rage that he'd half expected her to throw it to the ground and stamp on it. But of course, she was far too professional to do something like that.

Then his dragon had glimmered at him. He'd paused partway across the shop floor and glanced back to see his mate look around hastily, then drop the sign and grind it angrily under one boot.

Warmth pooled in his chest. *My mate.*

He cleared his throat. "I suppose I can see the value in it. Expensive books to display good taste or match the décor—"

Peony snorted. "What would you know about décor? There's literally nothing in your house that doesn't have a practical use."

He raised a careful eyebrow. He still wasn't sure how much of this was real and how much was a game, but God, he wouldn't stop playing it for the world. "You're not suggesting people actually still read books?"

"Of course they do!"

"Ebooks, maybe, but—"

"*Real* books." Peony paused and held up her hands placatingly. He got the feeling there was an old argument here she was used to making. "Not that ebooks aren't real books. I *love* ebooks. But there's a difference between handing over a gift card and letting someone fill their device, and giving someone a physical copy of a book that you know they'll love, or that you cherished from your childhood, or that has really *biteable* edges—"

"Excuse me?" Was this her inner cat coming through?

She grinned at him. "Board books for babies. Compelling reading material *and* something to chomp on, all in one."

"And better than letting them chew on your phone."

"Exactly!"

She hurried to the back of the store. Mordecai followed her, feeling . . . strange.

He was the dragon. So why did he feel like a wandering knight, creeping into a cave of treasures?

He had barely noticed his surroundings when he'd been in the building the night before. His attention had all been on his enemies. And then on Peony.

Trying desperately to be on anything but Peony, he corrected himself with a twist of guilt.

The store was dark. Light from outside filtered around the edges of the blinds that covered the big front windows, just enough to fill the shop floor with deep shadows instead of pitch black. Darkness made all the books anonymous. A thousand unreadable covers and spines.

He couldn't imagine anything less welcoming. And this was how his mate wanted to spend their first full day together?

What were you expecting? said a shiver-sharp voice inside

him. *Her to fall into your open arms? She'd have to wrench them open first.*

But they'd got past that, hadn't they? She still sniped at him, and he played the stuffy, sneering asshole, but . . . it was a game. Wasn't it?

Maybe she regrets last night. Or maybe it was part of the game, too.

Maybe she just hates you.

Ice formed inside him. "What is it we are doing here again? I can't help but notice that patrons aren't filling the streets, desperate to buy biteable books."

Peony glanced back at him, eyes wide. Her edges shimmered and—**Nononono-shit-not-now**—"Oh no. I am *not* shifting again. You're not getting out of this that easily!" She narrowed her eyes at him and disappeared behind a door. A moment later, the shop lights turned on, and the gloomy shelves transformed.

When Mordecai thought *bookstore*, if he thought of them at all, he thought of clinical white lights and enameled shelves of soulless bestsellers, or close-ranked, musty shelves beneath flickering, yellowed bulbs. This was neither. The overhead lights filled the shop with a warm glow. The front of the store had tables piled high with books, lit like the Crown Jewels, and shelving units were cunningly arranged around them to invite browsers to venture further into the store. *Do you like the look of these cookbooks?* they seemed to ask. *Just wait until you see what's back here. Or is it thrillers you're after? Romance? Dragons and wizards? Come and peruse my wares. You're going to love it here.*

The Christmas décor was still up, of course, but behind it, the shop's workaday wonder shone through. Even the light fixtures were in on it: soft pink roses hung from the pendant light above the romance section, and an origami dragon wound around the tops of the fantasy shelves, guarding the books. There was a taped outline of a body on the floor in the Crime section. It was whimsical and ridiculous, and he couldn't imagine Blanderley having signed off on any of it.

This all had to be Peony's doing.

Cluttered, he tried to tell himself as Peony hurried over to the big counter that took pride of place in the center of the store. *A dust trap. Who needs so many books anyway? Glued-up scraps of paper and cardboard full of stories that don't help anyone.*

There was a reason he kept his own rooms so bare. He didn't need the distraction. Why escape into a book when the real world was always waiting once you reached the last page?

He had one goal in life, and he couldn't afford to let anything into his life that gave him a hope of doing something else with it.

Mordecai blinked. *Where did that come from?*

His dragon shrugged, as lost as he was.

And across the room, Peony ran her fingers across the spines of a row of books. No longer shadowy and anonymous, but warmly lit and welcoming. *Not only stories,* he realized. *Whole worlds. And not only for escaping into. For sharing.*

This was what he was taking away from her. And in exchange for what? An apartment so impersonal her first impression of it was that it smelled dead. He could buy her a new house—he would have to because, even if she didn't hate his apartment, it was a bachelor's rooms, not . . .

Not a home. Not a *family* home.

Stillness washed through him, a cool chill that he wasn't sure was fear or awe. A family. He hadn't even considered . . . Peony was around thirty. She'd said she was waiting for her mate for her life to begin. Were children part of that life? Would she want—

"Come and help me with these, would you?" Peony called from across the room.

He came back to himself with a start. Those were all questions for later. After—

Christmas.

Dear god.

"These are all the remaining orders that haven't been picked up yet," Peony explained when he reached the counter. She worried her bottom lip, eyes flicking to the blinds that were still covering the windows. "I know some of our regulars will be in today to pick up books without ordering, but we don't have the staff to cover the desk *and* take these orders around. I can't ask anyone to come in after last night." Her features tightened briefly, then her usual problem-solving expression was back as though it had never left. Mordecai's chest twisted. "Though . . . I suppose . . ."

She cast her eye out over the store and dashed away, returning a few minutes later with another armload of books. "Help me wrap these? I might not be able to open the store, but I *can* take an educated guess about what our regularly last-minute customers might need, and do a home delivery."

Thirty minutes later, they were back in his car. Peony had a stack of books wrapped in festive paper bags on her lap and was peering at a list of addresses on her phone.

"Okay. First up . . ." She rattled off an address.

Mordecai dutifully plugged it into the GPS. "We could have walked," he pointed out.

"And risk your ankle again?" She grinned at him. "Besides, these are only the first deliveries. Not all our customers are local. Some of our regulars come from all across the city. Mrs. Nevis here is always telling me stories about when the Hypatia was still—" She broke off.

"Still . . .?" Mordecai prompted her.

Peony swallowed. A sense of confusion shivered down the connection between them, and Mordecai frowned.

"Still, you know. Properly running. People living in grand apartments upstairs, all the boarded-up shops downstairs still in use. Mrs. Nevis's grandmother used to take her to high teas at the restaurant when she was a little girl, but that must have been sixty or seventy years ago. She said there used to be a ballroom, too."

"And a swimming pool," Mordecai said absently. "The Riviera with central air and no sand to get between your toes."

"What?" Peony stared at him, eyes wide. "How do you know about that?"

He cursed himself silently. "My grandmother."

She didn't say anything. He cursed himself again. This was a tactic he often used—leaving a silence so deep and empty that your opponent rushed to fill it—and here he was, falling for it.

"My grandmother used to live in the Hypatia," he explained, jaw tight. "A long time ago."

"Huh." Peony looked out the window, her expression troubled. *She's figuring it out,* he thought and didn't understand why the thought made him feel so hopeless. "I guess I'll meet her tomorrow? And you'll meet my family. They're a few hours away. I usually drive down Christmas Eve, but I don't know if you'd prefer to split the day or do one family each year or—"

"I think it would be best if we got my family visit over as soon as possible."

Peony stared at him, mouth still open from him cutting her off. She closed it. Swallowed. He watched her digest the sharpness of his words. "That bad?" she asked, sympathetically. "If it helps, my family are going to love you."

Shit. "I didn't mean— My grandmother isn't the pleasantest company. Particularly around Christmas. It'll be no reflection on you."

"I wasn't worried about her not liking me," Peony murmured. **Believe it or not, I was trying to reassure you.**

The touch of her mind against his was too much. His jaw ached. "We could see my grandmother in the morning, then drive to visit your family for the rest of the day. If that works for you."

"Make 'em wait? I like it. Oh! Here's our stop."

Mordecai stayed with the car as Peony carted an armful of parcels to a nearby building. He watched as she buzzed the door, her breath coming out in white puffs.

Grandmother. Why had he mentioned her? If only he'd kept

his mouth shut, he could have . . .

Could have what? Avoided the subject forever? Pretended she didn't exist? He groaned. The ache in his jaw moved to the back of his head, tense and squeezing. *She's going to find out sooner or later.*

And as much as I might wish it would be later, it's going to be sooner.

The door opened. Peony greeted the person behind it cheerfully, and although he couldn't make out their conversation, he could imagine it. He saw the moment the customer asked what was happening to the bookstore. Peony went completely still. Then she burst out of the stillness like she was cracking through a thin film of ice, her reassurances too bright and too perky to be genuine.

When she came back towards the car, there was a moment when the brightness broke and uncertainty flooded up in its place. He tasted it on the very edge of the matebond before she locked it, and her expression, away again.

By the time the pile of books in his car was down to the last brightly colored parcel, he understood.

"Last stop." Peony's voice was as chirpy as it had been all afternoon, but it rang false. The hollow bit of Mordecai's chest ached. "I'll be a minute."

She raced out of the car and up to the building as though her heels were on fire. He tried to drag his eyes away from her but couldn't.

The tight line of her shoulders was clear even through her muffling winter jacket. Her cat form had pounced and scratched at him, and even when she'd shot barbs at him in human form, her body had moved with constant energy. She'd danced rings around him, sneaking closer and darting away, with an electric tantalizing intensity that had left his head spinning. And now she was stiff, jerky, as though her whole body was shutting down.

He'd gotten it all wrong.

This wasn't a game for her. She really had intended to give up the Hypatia.

And she was only now discovering what it meant to her. What she was really giving up.

She didn't know.

No wonder she had blown hot and cold, fighting against him and herself at the same time.

She hadn't known how precious the bookstore was to her until he'd come to take it away. Hadn't known how much she loved herself or the life she was already living until he kissed her and took it all away.

His mate had spent her whole life waiting to meet him and find out who she truly was. And now she had, and it was tearing her apart.

How? How can anyone live like that? He couldn't imagine having something so important in his life and not knowing it for what it was. His revenge had fueled him since he was a child. He'd always known what he would do with his life. The destruction of the Hypatia was his guiding star. To not have that direction . . . or to have it but not recognize what it was until it was gone . . .

And she was going to let him. No wonder anger and anguish had flared from her like the last sparks of a dying fire. She thought her newly emerged inner animal meant she was small and weak and had to fold herself into his life. His plans. His revenge.

Until she snuffed out everything that burned so fiercely inside her.

Scales crawled over his skin as his dragon moved uneasily. *Our fault?*

He bit back a sigh. His ankle sent him a ghostly twinge, a pretend echo of a pretend injury. *Not your fault,* he told his dragon gently. Wanting his mate was as natural as breathing, or lifting his face to feel the morning sun. He couldn't blame the creature for throwing them both into Peony's path.

But he could blame himself for everything that had happened since.

Light glowed around Peony as someone opened the door. He watched her greet the other person, exchange small talk, wave excitedly to someone farther inside, and hand over the bag of giftwrapped books . . . and then brace herself before she turned and came back down the steps.

"Peony," he said as she sat down, and he caught a whisper of *Help, he's using the disappointed Victorian schoolmaster voice.*

And a hint of arousal, which confused him.

"We should talk," he went on, and her eyebrows shot up.

"Correction: we should eat," she retorted breezily. "I'm not facing a 'we should talk' conversation on an empty stomach, and that nutritional smoothie turned to fumes hours ago."

She made an excellent point. "I'll call for a table at—"

"No." She still had her hood up, and now she peered at him from under it, her brown face like a pixie staring out at him from inside some sort of fluffy flower. "Come on. Really?"

"Really what?"

"We're not getting a *table* anywhere. We're going to do the thing." She got out of the car and started hurrying down the street.

He followed her, confused. "What—"

"The *Christmas* thing. Come on, Mr. Sad-Eyes. After what you said about your grandmother, I think you're well overdue some Christmas cheer, of the tinsel-est, carol-est sort available." She danced her fingers at the street ahead, where a sign claimed they were approaching the Featherwell Christmas Market.

When Mordecai had plugged the last delivery location into the GPS, the map had shown this street in bright red: impassable. Now he saw why. The whole street and the plaza beyond was blocked up to make space for a huge Christmas market.

"This is perfect. Ice-skating! Hot cocoa! Look—I'm pretty sure they recycled that booth from the haunted house market at Halloween. Maybe we can even get someone to rustle us up some Christmas ghosts."

"I take it I'm the Scrooge in this situation."

"I didn't say that." She trapped his arm in hers. "Come *on*."

He could have argued. He could have planted his feet on the sidewalk and refused to move. The timer in his head was ticking closer and closer to zero. He was running out of time to figure out how to make things right.

Especially now he knew just how wrong they were.

But then Peony shot him a grin that was pure mischief, and tugged him towards the Halloween-esque ticket booth. The bright-eyed reindeer either side of the entranceway had a distinctly demonic look.

"I thought Rudolph had a red nose, not glowing red eyes," he muttered to Peony, who giggled.

"Pretty sure the Santa behind them was the Headless Horseman last time I saw him."

"He's looking good for a corpse." Mordecai paid for the entry tickets and frowned as the ticket seller handed him a map. "What sort of a market needs a map?"

Peony raised one eyebrow at him. "You've never been to the Featherwell Market before?"

"What sort of a name is *Featherwell*?" He avoided answering her question because he didn't know how to tell the truth in a way that wasn't depressing.

He usually spent the Christmas season preparing for Christmas dinner with his grandmother and then recovering from it. The last thing he would have done any other year was remind himself of how other people's Christmases went by visiting a celebration like this.

"They used to make pillows here. Proper duck-down ones." Peony plucked the map from his hands and unfolded it. "But there wasn't a lot of space, so instead of duck ponds, they kept the ducks in wells."

"You're making that up."

"No, why would you think that?" She turned the map

around a few times. "Think about it. Instead of spreading the ducks over the flat surface of a pond—such an inefficient use of space—you pack them into a well and make the most of your square footage. Ooh, candy apples!"

"I refuse to believe anyone stacked ducks in wells here at any time in history."

Peony shrugged. "Suit yourself."

A dozen steps into the market, and Mordecai suddenly understood why they needed a map. This wasn't the quaint scattering of stalls he'd imagined; it was a miniature town. Food and craft stalls crammed together like something out of Dickens. The walkways between them were more like alleyways, twisting and turning. Cider donuts, mulled wine, funnel cakes, some sort of potato twist on a stick—one turn and he'd never find his way out again.

Why find our way out when there's so much here to eat and share with our mate? his dragon asked, confused.

Peony nudged him. "What do you think? Lunch, hot cocoa, games, and then shopping?"

"Shopping?"

"Well, yeah." To his surprise, she looked nervous. "Christmas is tomorrow. You're going to have to meet my family. And like I said, they're going to be extremely excited to meet you. It'll be a lot. I recommend bringing enough gifts to throw at them and run away if it gets too bad."

"Sounds like a sensible precaution."

She relaxed. "I'm glad you think so. Food is always good. Toffee. If their teeth are stuck together, they can't ask horribly invasive questions."

They're not shifters? Toffee-jammed teeth wouldn't stop a shifter from asking questions.

Peony's face fell. "Oh. I didn't think about that." She rallied quickly but seemed unusually shaken. "Toffee for the mind, then. What would that be? Alcohol? If they're too sloshed to think straight, they can't ask too many questions, right?"

"Let me see the map. Hmm. I don't see a listing for the festive vodka stall."

"No? Usually it's right next to the duck wells." Peony's nose wrinkled as she grinned. "What about your family? Should I be loading up on artillery gifts for them as well?"

"God, no. There's only one thing my grandmother wants, and I've already organized it." He didn't realize how bitter the words would come out until he'd already spoken them.

"Um. Okay. Point taken." She winced. "There's nothing I can get her? Not even a good book? My budget isn't exactly endless, but . . ."

"It's not a case of you not being able to afford something appropriate." *Well done, Mr. Smooth.* "We don't normally do gifts."

"And . . . it's only your grandmother?"

"She's my only family, yes." *Should he say more? Yes,* his dragon nudged him. *Explain. How else is she going to understand?*

Mordecai imagined a future in which he told Peony everything, about his victory and why she was paying the price for it, and she treated him exactly as he deserved.

I'm too much of a coward.

"I'm sorry," she said.

"Don't be. My life is hardly a tragedy."

"All right." She squeezed his arm. It was barely a touch—a moment of pressure through layers of thick fabric—but it left him warm and strange-feeling. "You're welcome to borrow as many of my relatives as you like, if you ever feel you're running low. I have cousins and aunts and uncles and this and that how many times removed coming out my ears."

"I'll keep that in mind," he said dryly.

Peony laughed. "Good. Okay. I think I've figured out the best route." She dragged her finger along the map. "Stuff ourselves with food here. Roll around the game stalls and lose all our money throwing balls at giant advent calendars and wobbling around on ice-skates. Shopping at the end, because first, that means less distance to carry everything back to the car, and second, we already lost all our money on the games, so we'll be stealing everything and running away."

"No doubt using the duck wells as our escape route."

"How'd you guess?"

She dragged him deeper into the market. He did his best to pay for everything, but every time he turned around, Peony was passing him a new winter treat to try or handing him a ball to throw at a knock-'em-down game. They gorged on donuts and chocolates and fried cheese and sausages, and pored over trinkets.

He kept waiting for the other shoe to drop. It was all too good to be true. *She must be putting it on*, he told himself when she hooted with laughter as her ball almost hit the stallholder instead of the toy on the shelf she'd aimed it at. *It must be an act*, as she snorted into her mug of mulled wine.

She can't really be this happy.

She put her arm around his again and pulled him towards the next stall.

It can't be me that's making her this happy.

He didn't deserve it. He didn't deserve her.

When the second shoe dropped, he was ready for it. They were near the end of the market, according to the map, only a few twisted corners away from the exit nearest where he had parked.

Peony was clutching bags around herself like armor. She turned to him. "There *is* something I'd like to talk to you about," she said and tilted her chin up to look him in the eye.

"Here?" *In public? In the middle of the most confusingly and overwhelmingly Christmas experience of my life?*

"Close." She reached out for him, hesitated, then took his arm. "At the ice-skating rink."

11

PEONY

Every idea Peony had was the worst, and yet she kept on having them.

Her heart was in her throat as she waited for Mordecai's answer. Part of her wanted him to say no. She wanted his eyes to blaze and his voice to go frosty and for him to reject this new, idiot scheme that her new cat-brained self had decided on.

But please say yes, she said, careful to keep her voice silent inside her own head. *Please, please say yes. I don't think I can manage this conversation without any distractions.*

"Ice-skating," he said at last. His voice didn't blaze, or crackle over with ice. Was that bad? "Very well."

Peony loved ice-skating. She told Mordecai so, as they waited in line for tickets and skate rental, and tried not to feel as though she was babbling.

"We always skated at home in winter," she said. "Whenever I tell people that now, they talk about how dangerous it sounds, skating on a pond in the middle of nowhere, and sure, it's all very *Little Women*, but . . ." She switched to telepathy. **Beth didn't have a flying deer babysitting her, or a kelpie cousin hanging out under the ice ready to boot her out if she fell in.** They both had their skates now; she sat down on a bench and began to take off her boots. "Really, the worst that could happen was being late for dinner. Which we always were. Dad *hated* that."

"He's the cook in your family?"

"Oh, yeah. Mom bakes, Dad cooks, the rest of us wash up. We all pitched in to try and buy them a dishwasher one year. Didn't work. Washing up is a sacred task, apparently, not to be fobbed off on mere appliances. Anyway, ice-skating . . ."

They were rink-side, now.

She put one skate on the ice. It was nasty, scarred-up fairground rink ice, but it still sent a thrill through her. *It always felt like flying to me. It made me wonder if my inner animal would have wings, too.*

"And now you know it doesn't?"

Why the hell wouldn't he respond to her telepathically? If anyone was listening in, the two of them would sound mad, their conversation full of weird pauses and answers to questions nobody asked.

She sighed and pushed out onto the ice. *Well, it doesn't matter, does it? Regardless, I'll still have ice-skating, and if I ever want to know what it's like to actually fly, I'll OH GOD OH GOD I HATE THIS, WHAT IS HAPPENING??? MY FEET??? MY FEET ARE SLIPPERY???*

Mordecai moved across the ice like a striking snake, intercepting her before she flailed into the path of a group of small children. *What happened? Are you all right?*

FEET??? SLIPPERY??? her cat wailed. She clamped one hand over her mouth. Which didn't help, of course it didn't help, because her cat had taken over her *mind,* not her mouth.

"I'm sorry," she blurted out. "It's . . . not used to—"

"Of course." Mordecai pulled her close against his side, his arm sure and strong around her waist. All the breath left her in a rush. Her feet scrabbled on the ice—*Not my fault,* she wanted to tell him, *I'm GOOD at ice-skating, this is EMBARRASSING*—but he was holding her so firmly that she didn't fall.

She was safe. He was keeping her safe.

Do you get that, you crazy little freak? she yelled at her cat. *We're safe! Nothing's wrong! Stop freaking out!*

WHY ARE WE SKIDDING? it yowled back. She—or her cat, oh *god,* she was never going to live this down—grabbed Mordecai with both arms and dug her fingers into his coat like they were claws.

He drew her closer and whispered in her ear, "What's that you were saying about loving ice-skating? You seem to be having a little trouble."

The *bastard.* "I—"

At the same moment, her cat went rigid with outrage. *What? Who's having trouble? We're not having trouble. Everything is fine here. Everything is horrible and fine.*

And it went limp.

Peony sagged against Mordecai. He chuckled and guided them both to the Christmas tree in the middle of the rink. A waist-high railing surrounded the tree, and he leaned her against it. *Better?*

She looked up into his eyes. He stared back—not with suspicion or impatience or lost in the heat of lust, but with concern.

Better, she confirmed. And at the touch of her mind to his, the echo of the word he'd placed in her head like a golden offering, he retreated.

Her head snapped back like he'd slapped her. "Do you even like me?" she blurted out.

He frowned. "What?"

"We keep talking about . . . about Christmas, and our families, like this is just going to *happen*. But this is the first time you've actually touched me. And it was . . . why? So I wouldn't fall over and embarrass you?"

His eyes darkened. "No, that's not . . . and this isn't the first time I've touched you."

An image rose unbidden in her mind: his hands on her body as she rode him. From the sudden heat in his gaze, the sudden tautness of the connection between them, he was thinking the same thing.

She shook her head sharply. *That doesn't count. The first time you've touched me without me touching you first. You know it's true. I kiss you, I touch you, I goddamn throw myself at you . . . If I didn't, would you do anything to me?*

All the control she'd leashed around her heart fell loose. She couldn't stop her emotions pouring down the matebond. All her twisted-up fears and hopes. She couldn't stop them, and she couldn't look at him anymore, either. Her gaze skittered sideways, to the glittering lights hanging from the ice-rink Christmas tree. They gleamed and ran together as tears filled her eyes.

You said you regretted walking away. But this hurts just as much. You won't even speak telepathically to me unless there's no other option. It's like you can't bear me to be in your mind. And I—my cat—likes the chase. But not if that's all there is. I can't always be the one closing the gap between us. She swallowed, trying and failing to wrench her emotions back under control. *I know neither of us chose this. But if there's something you'd rather I do—something you'd find sexier, or more palatable, or—*

"No. Don't say that."

The shock in his voice shook her. She took a shaking breath, then another, then forced herself to meet his eyes again.

Slowly, he raised one hand to her cheek. *I'm sorry,* he said, the touch of his mind gentler than snowflakes. *I didn't realize I was hurting you. I will do better.* He brushed a tear from her cheek.

Why? she asked.

Because I do want you. I would choose you, choose this, a thousand times over. His eyes narrowed as he searched her face, and a muscle twitched at the corner of his mouth. *I don't want you always to be the one pursuing me, either.*

Then why do you never reach out? Why is it always me pestering you?

I don't want to hurt you. I want so much from you, and it is unfair of me to want so much when I've already taken everything from you. I shouldn't ask more of you until I have more to offer.

Something twisted inside her. "You haven't taken anything from me," she said.

"No?" His eyebrow rose, sardonic. "Your job? Your apartment? The life you'd built for yourself, waiting for me to turn up?"

"That's not . . . It's not important." She stumbled over the words.

He sighed. "Of course."

What does that mean? Her heart was in her throat again.

Before she could ask, Mordecai cupped her face in his hand. "I will do better," he promised. "Starting now."

He kissed her, and everything else in the world fell away. She sank into his embrace, all her fears and the sick, helpless feeling inside dropping from her shoulders like a heavy cloak. She was free and light and wanted.

Everything was going to be okay.

And with regards to you not always being the one who does the chasing . . . He let the statement drift in her mind, tantalizingly unfinished.

She opened her eyes, kiss-dazed, and the heat in his gaze made her toes curl. "Oh?" she said, helpfully.

"Hmm," he said. Equally helpful. Maybe they were a good match, after all.

She took a tentative step backwards, easing along the ice. He followed her. She glided farther away. He stalked after her, tall and dark, a black-winged bird against the cheerful brightness of the lights and the white-shining ice.

What is he? What was her mate's inner animal? Something wonderful. Something powerful and strong and *hers*.

But it doesn't matter even if he is a frog. So long as he's mine.

She slipped away over the ice, and he followed, always a step behind. She spun in a slow arc; he swung after her, a pendulum on a chain soldered directly over her heart. Her pulse quickened. On the next arc, he caught her arm.

They spun together for a heartbeat, then sprang apart. She sped up—he closed the gap between them, pulled her into a whirl of an embrace, and let her go again so fast she almost thought she'd imagined the pressure of his lips against hers.

Her heart lurched after him as he let the distance between them stretch unbearably long, then he was after her again and she couldn't get away fast enough. His arms closed around her, strong and possessive, and she never wanted him to let go.

His breath was hot against her ear. "We should find somewhere more private."

They were back in his apartment. Mordecai had barely let go of her the whole drive back. His hand on her arm, her shoulder, her thigh. His touch searing. His gaze even hotter.

She walked backwards until she hit a wall. He planted his hands either side of her. Penning her in.

"Tell me what you want," he pleaded, his voice a broken growl, and her heart kicked behind her ribs. "Whatever you want me to do. Tell me."

He kissed her before she could answer.

This, she breathed into his mind, hands tangled in his hair as the rest of her went loose and hot. *Show me you're as crazy about me as I am about you.* She wanted him helpless and heartlost with lust for her. Didn't he want the same?

Yes. He pinned her against the wall, his body hard against hers.

"Then it sounds like our interests align." Her voice wasn't as dry as she wanted, imitating him—too throaty, too needy—but Mordecai groaned and moved against her, and nothing else mattered.

"I want to see you go to pieces." His voice was a burr against her neck, her collarbone, her lips. "I want to make you cry out my name. I want to make you feel the way you made me feel. Like you'd given me the world."

Was that what she'd done? She'd claimed him like a cavewoman dragging him back to her cave by the hair. She'd made him *hers*, spun his pleasure tight and taut with her body and sent him spiraling over the edge.

"*Yes*," he moaned again, in her head and against her skin. "Like that."

"I want more than that." She grabbed his head and looked into his eyes so that *she* couldn't look away. He wanted to know what she wanted, so she had to be brave enough to say it. "I want you every way there is. I want you to fuck me so hard I never forget the feeling of you inside me." And then, swift on the heels of that particular statement, as though she could slip it in while he was still reeling, "I want you in my head, Mordecai, and I want to be in yours."

Wickedness danced in his broken-glass eyes. *Like this?*

Mordecai touched her mind with his, and there was nothing she wanted more than for that moment to last forever. Lights flickered behind her eyes. Her toes curled, and she pressed herself against him, dove into his kiss as though by kissing him she could hold him there forever, the shadow-whisper of his thoughts brushing against hers.

Want.

Desire.

Need.

It flooded through her until she didn't know which thoughts were hers and which were his. Crackling fire need and roaring floodwater need and, oh god, if he didn't touch her more, she was going to *scream.*

"Is that a promise?" His breath teased her ear.

She moaned, not bothering to hide it anymore. "We'll see."

Another surprised *ha.* She slid one hand into his shirt, her fingers slipping into the gaps between buttons. He wasn't wearing an undershirt. His chest was firm and muscular, and his heart beat like a drum beneath her touch.

She dragged at the top button until it snapped off. He grumbled something.

"What? You bought me a whole new wardrobe and you're worrying about a button?" *Snap.* There went another one.

She felt *drunk.* Was this what being mated was like? Being drunk all the time, off her whiskey-smoke mate? She could live with that.

"I'm contributing to the local economy," she suggested. *Pop.* "Creating jobs."

Ohhh my god. Seeing his chest was even better than feeling it. He had a sprinkling of dark hair, just enough to tug on—which she did, gleefully—and the *muscles.* All that skin.

Why hadn't she done this the first time? What kind of an

idiot let a man like this keep his shirt on while she was fucking him?

The heat coming off him was almost scorching; she was surprised the air around him wasn't hazy with mirage like a hot street on an even hotter day.

Pop.

She'd almost run out of buttons.

Mordecai grabbed her hand as it hovered over the final button.

She raised her eyebrows at him. "Sorry? Do you not want to contribute to the local economy?"

"I want to know what I'm getting myself into." Forget necromancer. With his shirt buttonless and falling off him and his scowling, broken-glass eyes, he looked like a grumpy pirate.

"Do I need to make it more obvious? Should I prepare a PowerPoint presentation?" She pressed herself against him. A *horny* grumpy pirate. *Wow.*

He lifted her hand to his lips and kissed her fingers. "I mean, are we going to have a furry problem?"

"What???"

"This could all be a trick." His kiss turned into a bite—gentle, but with enough teeth in it to make her insides melt. "You want me vulnerable, again. Do I need to worry about you transforming, again?"

She narrowed her eyes. "You're seriously asking this? Now?"

"Very seriously."

"What, you're suddenly worried about claws near your delicate parts?"

"Ye—" He looked at her suspiciously. Which was sensible. Her smile was very suspect. Like the Cheshire Cat. "Let me rephrase." He narrowed his eyes even further. "I am as concerned as it is possible for me to be without your cat seeing it as a challenge."

Am I that transparent?

"Yes," he said shortly.

She danced her fingers down his bare chest. "And if I can't guarantee I won't accidentally explode into a pint-sized ball of fluff and knife-like talons?"

His lips twitched.

"Should *I* be worried? About you suddenly exploding into . . . whatever your inner animal looks like?"

"That would be disastrous. Luckily, of the two of us, I'm the one who has shown the most control over his animal form so far."

"Disastrous how? Worse than claws near your cock? Piercing damage to your pe—"

"*Stop.*"

"If I'm willing to risk disaster, you should be able to risk me turning into a tiny fluffy cat." She paused with her fingers at the edge of his pants. He was hot and hard against her. Unyielding.

Unravel. Please. Or at least unbend, for me, even a little. Show me that you're as lost in this as I am.

She didn't know if he'd heard her or not. But something in his face softened.

He traced a line down her cheek, her jawbone, dipping beneath her chin. "Touché," he murmured.

She licked her lips. "You survived last time, anyway."

"I did."

"If I think I'm at risk of shifting again, I'll just think human thoughts."

"What sort of human thoughts? In case I need to coach you through it."

"Taxes." He didn't believe her. "Utility bills."

"Tell me what you really thought of." His voice caressed her, touching all her most sensitive places. "Tell me what made you need your human form again so badly."

"You."

He slid his hands under the hem of her dress and pulled it up, over her hips, over her belly, up to her breasts. She arched towards him as he cupped a breast, his thumb brushing over the nipple.

Was he *rewarding* her? For answering his question?

That was . . . really fucking hot, actually.

"I'm going to need more detail than that."

"You, doing taxes . . ."

Mordecai bared his teeth in a laugh against her skin. Her heart skipped a beat. "Liar."

"I wanted to see what you looked like if I tore the buttons off your shirt."

His hand seared a path down her side, fingers flaring out wide as he reached her hips. She was wearing thick woolen tights, the least sensual item in the entire wardrobe he'd bought her. Or so she'd thought until he started pulling them down, inch by inch. "And?"

"I wanted—" She broke off on a gasp as he kissed her belly. *You're my mate.* She sent the words through the mysterious bond that connected her soul to his. *The first time I saw you, I went hot and cold with wanting you. Then I got to take you back to my apartment, and kissing you seemed like the obvious next worst thing to do on the worst evening ever.*

Her heart hiccupped. She hadn't meant to confess that. But Mordecai continued his slow, sensual exploration of her body.

Should she look into his mind? Try to see whether she'd offended him, or— No.

She took a deep breath. *And then . . . you were my mate.*

His lips brushed the hem of her panties. She wriggled, trying to get closer—him to her, or herself to him, either, anything—but he put his hands on her hips and held her in place.

Desire spiked through her. Oh yes, right now *this* was what she wanted, him taking her, overwhelming her with how much she needed him, but not letting her do anything about it until he wanted it.

I know, his voice purred into her mind. *But I asked you a question.*

Of all the maddening, sexy, hot assholes in the world, of course this one had to be hers.

"Yes, yes," he whispered, oh-god-so-close to her clit but holding her so tight she couldn't even buck against him. "Do try to concentrate."

"*You,*" she gasp-moaned. "I was trying so hard not to think about you. Because it was all so much. My cat. Being a shifter. My whole future had changed, and I wasn't as ready for it as I thought I was. But then I thought . . . you. Kissing you meant I *had* to be a tiny fluffy cat, but it meant I *got* to have you."

Mordecai muttered something wonderful and filthy against the crease of her thigh.

"And I needed to be human for that."

He swore, dark and icy and *hers,* and buried his face between her legs.

His tongue flicked out, seeking, finding, tasting, and every nerve in her body sang out in chorus. *More! More!* She twisted and squirmed against his grip, and he lifted her until only her tiptoes were touching the floor.

And now? His voice left sparks of lightning in her mind.

She let her head drop back and moaned. **Kissing you turned out to be the best idea of my life.**

She gasped aloud as he thrust his tongue inside her. He was ravenous and gentle at the same time, a combination that left her head spinning and everything else in her tightening to a single exquisite point.

"I'm so close." Her voice was a ragged whisper. "I'm so close, I—"

Her toes left the ground. She wrapped one leg over his shoulder and braced her other foot against the wall, scrabbling for purchase as pleasure jolted through her.

Good? Mordecai's voice was a tease, the sly touch of his tongue on her again an even worse one, and she was too breathless and weak-legged to respond in kind.

She'd just come on his face. She'd just . . . wow. And he was still holding her, firmly and worshipfully, as though he knew if he let go she would fall into a puddle on the floor.

What else?

"Uhh?" she said, sexily. He turned his face and laughed into the crease of her leg again. Oh god, she could live in this moment forever. Mordecai laughing. Mordecai holding her, caressing her, wanting her and taking her and not letting her go.

He sighed raggedly. "I should have done this from the start."

"Yes. Yes. Definitely. Yes." There. She'd said words. Whole words.

Well done, he murmured dryly.

Blame yourself. Telepathy was easier than convincing her mouth to make words. Especially since it turned out her psychic safeguards weren't guarding her thoughts as safely as they were meant to. *I want you to keep doing that until I can't even think whole words, let alone say them.*

There. She'd dangled the bait.

He took it, and her with it.

Mordecai rose up like a demon in front of her, hair tangled, eyes like blazing stars, mouth wet from . . . *from me, holy shit, wet from ME.* He kissed her, and she tasted herself on his lips and his hunger in her mind.

Mine, her cat said at that hint of Mordecai's mind in her own. It chased the ghost of him—hot whiskey and sweet, rich caramel—as he picked her up, and she barely noticed him carrying her to the bedroom, too lost in the touch of her mate's lips and tongue and soul to pay attention to the outside world.

Until her back hit the mattress and he was on top of her.

"Tell me again," he whispered rawly, his body all heat and

hardness and coiled, sensuous power above her. "Tell me what you want until you can't tell me in words anymore."

She didn't even bother with words then. She sent her desire straight into his mind. *Touch me. Hold me. Hard and fast and NOW.*

He growled, even more wordless than he'd mocked her for being, and she told him that, too, as he pulled her dress up over her head and ran his hands over her body. She'd been naked in front of him yesterday, but this was different, this was *better*, because he wasn't holding back anymore. His desire for her flooded her mind. Each touch echoed through her—her own sensation, then his lust and wonder, blazing through the matebond like wildfire.

His pants were gone. She wound herself around him, body and soul, exploring every inch of his bare skin as he covered her with kisses. How had she denied herself all this, not stripping him off last night? He was glorious. Under his hands, his lips, she felt glorious, too.

She'd wanted touch; this was worship.

You deserve to be worshipped. His mouth was at her breast; he looked up at her, dark eyes sharp and glinting. *You deserve a mate who'll give you everything you want.*

I want you, she told him. Her mind curled out, reaching for his. *Oh.* He let her in again, the breathless rush of intimacy almost too much. Something huge and scaly whirled overhead, just behind the corners of her eyes, gone before she could more than glimpse it.

Then she found the walls within his mind.

They were tall, dark, and forbidding, rising up beyond where she could see. She reached out, placing one hand against them. Her cat-self scratched, curiously, and he shuddered.

I can't— His voice broke off, ragged-edged, but he didn't draw back. *I want to give you everything. I want to make you happy. But I can't make myself anything but what I am. This is why I couldn't touch you first, before. Because if I show you who I really am, you won't want me anymore.*

Who you really are?

Grief and wistful regret whirled around her. *A monster. A villain. But I can still give you this.*

He positioned himself above her. His weight anchored her soul; all her tumbling, flying thoughts and desires funneled in on this. On *him*.

She strained towards him. "I want—"

I know.

He thrust into her. She gripped him with her legs, holding him fully sheathed inside her, and *clenched*. He swore, his breath hot against her neck, and thrust again, driving her into the mattress. She met him movement for movement, writhing against him, until he held her down.

Yes.

Pinned her with his weight.

Yes!

More, she told him silently. *Body and soul. Everything. All of you. Villainy and all.*

Yes, his soul cried out to hers, and she came undone. Pleasure rushed through her as she came, and her clenching, keening orgasm dragged him along with it. He came with a shuddering gasp, and she clutched at him, not wanting to lose one moment of his touch.

Her mind reached deeper into his, and the walls she'd scratched against were gone.

One heartbeat of shock: *He let me in.*

And then the storm of ice that had been locked away behind the walls crashed over her.

A chasm gaped open inside her, as though the storm Mordecai had kept locked away was scouring her own soul empty. She pushed forward. What was this? How could this be what he'd been hiding behind his impenetrable walls?

He *pretended* to be cold-hearted, but she'd seen past that mask already. She knew he could be warm and careful and kind. *Where is it?*

Then she saw it, deep within the storm and the emptiness that howled all around. And she understood.

I want her to be happy. His voice wrapped around her like a cloak, ragged-edged and raw. *But how can she be happy when I'm like this?*

The emptiness. The loneliness. A whole lifetime of wanting one thing, and it had almost lost him the only thing that mattered.

Oh, Mordecai, she thought, her own heart breaking.

He wanted so desperately to be hers, and he thought she wouldn't have him.

She made her decision.

You do make me happy, she told him, and wrapped herself

around the cold, lonely core of him.

"Peony?" The shaking in his voice made her open her eyes. He was staring down at her, his gaze half-wild, half-hopeful. "You . . ."

"It's true." She touched his face, tracing the deep lines of stress around his eyes and mouth until they eased. "You're mine, Mordecai. And I'm not going to let you go."

He fell onto her. And when she'd come again and thought that was all she had left, he took her again, and again, until any doubt she'd had that he wanted her was a distant memory.

They showered. Ate. Fell into bed again. Ate. *Threw* themselves into bed again. Peony lost and recovered her ability to form words so many times she lost count. Their lovemaking became less urgent. Slower, languid, a relaxation into each other's bodies, a gentle caress of mind to mind like the lap of water against the shore.

And then something changed.

They were still connected, physically and mentally. He closed his eyes—one last pretense that there were any walls between them? Then he looked down at her, his gaze as fiercely possessive as before, but grim, as well.

What now? Tension ratcheted along her spine.

"This wasn't how I expected today to go," he admitted. He ran one lazy hand down her side and rested it on her hip. A gentle worship, after the urgency of their lovemaking. "When I sensed your unhappiness and asked you to tell me what you wanted, I was waiting for you to make different demands of me."

He hesitated, and something like dread curled in her stomach at the watchfulness in his eyes. "What?"

"I thought you were going to ask me for your old life back."

She snorted. "What life? Maybe if I'd made something of my life before you, I would have regretted leaving it behind now that I'm a shifter—"

"What about the Hypatia?"

Her heart lurched. She lifted her chin. "What about it? I've left it behind. You have your own plans for it, anyway, and they're . . ."

She swallowed. Swallowed again. Why was this so hard to say?

She had everything she wanted. A mate who made her deliriously happy. An inner animal who wasn't as helpless and pathetic as she'd feared, even if it was a tiny fluffball. And a future full of . . . of . . .

"You don't have to pretend." Mordecai's voice was infuriatingly gentle.

"I'm not pretending! The Hypatia doesn't mean anything to me. It *can't*."

12

MORDECAI

Peony's certainty wavered.

"It *can't*." She drew a deep breath. "You have your own thing going on with the Hypatia, and I *can't* get in the way of that. Not when it's so important to you."

Her words struck him like a blow to the chest.

All the time he'd been watching her, trying to figure out the mystery that was his beautiful, clever, troubled mate, she'd been doing the same to him.

And she'd figured him out.

"I'm right, aren't I?" Her eyes dipped, then rose to meet his, warm and incisive. "The Hypatia isn't just a random target for you. You want to destroy it *specifically*. Not shut it down or renovate it or repurpose it. Destroy it."

"I should have known better than to hide anything from you."

She made a short, explosive noise. "Just because I can't keep my thoughts hidden doesn't mean you need to give up all privacy in this relationship. You have your reasons for wanting to demolish the Hypatia, and I . . . I don't have any real reasons for wanting to keep it as it is."

Her voice was normal. But the words were all wrong. And

the glowing connection between them—it was dull. Subdued.

Something fought in her eyes for a moment, and then it was gone. "I *don't*," she said again.

Mordecai's dragon chittered its teeth. *Something's wrong.*

Yes. I can see that.

"That's all? You're giving in?" He waited for her to say, *Don't sound so disappointed.* She didn't. "No mad last-minute schemes? You're not going to lure me into a back alley and threaten me with a tire iron until I swear not to demolish the Hypatia?"

She winced slightly at the building's name but still didn't say anything.

A pit opened in the bottom of Mordecai's stomach. "Peony—"

"Can we stop talking about it? I'm not going to bother you about that anymore." She lay back with an exasperated sigh, but the part of her soul that still touched his—that he hoped always would touch his—was cold and brittle. The pit in his stomach deepened. "Today . . . I tied up all the loose ends. All the final Christmas orders. Everything else is admin."

"You're clenching your fists."

She looked down at her hands as though she was surprised to see them. Her fingers relaxed one by one, as though she was having to convince them. "This is the first day of the rest of my life. I need to start acting like it. Time to grow up."

The last words were little more than a whisper, but he could feel the blade in them. Aimed directly at herself.

"And what does growing up look like, exactly?"

"I don't know?" She gestured vaguely. "Being your mate.

Drinking horrible smoothies. Not . . . not worrying about things that shouldn't matter to me. Like I said before, maybe if I'd made something of myself before I met you, things would be different, but . . ."

"Don't say that."

She bared her teeth at him. "I love it when you snap at me. My villainous mate."

"You did make something of your life. You may not have meant to, but you did."

"Well." She looked away. "It's too late to worry about that now. What time is it? Shouldn't we be planning for tomorrow? If we visit your grandmother in the morning—"

"I never wanted to destroy the Hypatia."

Peony frowned. For a moment, she didn't believe him, and then without even searching his mind, she did. She stared at him, bristling with curiosity. "What do you mean?"

She's seen into the deepest part of my soul. The weakest part of me. And she didn't reject it.

I need to tell her.

"Destroying the Hypatia isn't my revenge. It was my grandmother's. Her family built it. It was my great-grandfather's grand gift to us all—a home to live in, with apartments and communal rooms big enough for our other forms. If we couldn't fly, here in the city, we could at least lie beneath the stained-glass canopies and pretend we were lounging under starlight instead of electric bulbs." He sighed.

"You . . . you *want* that. I felt it."

His mouth twisted wryly. "It surprises me, too. I haven't

allowed myself to feel anything about the building except as something to destroy for . . . for a long time."

"You said your grandmother took you somewhere underground to wait for your inner animal to emerge. Was that the Hypatia? No," she got in before he could answer. "The timeline doesn't match up."

"The Hypatia had been lost to our family for decades by the time I first shifted. But the first time my grandmother described it to me, I wanted it." He laughed humorlessly. "She soon cured me of that."

"And you never let yourself want it again." She narrowed her eyes at him. "No wonder there was a storm raging inside you."

"What better way to ignore my own conflicted feelings than to hide them away where even I could not interrogate them?" He grimaced again. She leaned against him, warm and soft and reassuring. "My great-grandparents had their family late. Grandmother was still young when they died and left the building to her. And she found her mate young. And lost him young, too."

"You said your grandmother is your only family."

"Tragedy upon tragedy. Your soul has picked an unlucky family to connect itself to."

She took his hand in hers. "No. I'm lucky to have found you."

"My grandmother lost everyone she loved. Maybe if she hadn't, she would be a different person. But she let her business advisers manage the Hypatia, and they took advantage of her grief to take the one thing she had left. And then they let it fall into ruin, as though it meant nothing."

"That's awful." Peony bent her head against his shoulder, then looked up at him. "But she hadn't lost everyone. She still had you."

"I . . . do not believe she saw it that way. Later, I was a useful tool. Once my shifter abilities emerged, I could forge myself into someone who could help her achieve her revenge. Before that . . ." He shook his head.

Cold crept beneath his skin.

He looked down at Peony. The cold was coming from her—and behind it, a trembling, red-hot rage that made the last traces of the storm inside him vanish.

"I was wrong about the Christmas orders being the final loose end to deal with. Forget waiting until tomorrow to see your grandmother," she snapped. "I want to meet her now."

🦇 🜚 🦇

It was dark by the time they arrived at his grandmother's apartment building.

Peony's nose twitched as they looked up at it. "This is where she lives? I think I looked at a place in this building when I first moved to the city." Her rage was still simmering, a reassuring warmth around his soul, but as she frowned up at the building, it was joined by confusion.

"Perhaps if you had, we would have met sooner. This is where I grew up." He joined her, staring up at the dark, shabby building. "She refused to let me move her anywhere better until the Hypatia was back in her hands."

"And then what? She was going to go squat in the rubble?"

He sensed her cat in the way she pinned the building with her gaze, but not the playful creature who'd tormented him—this was something fiercer and more intent. Protective.

Protective of me. He felt guilty at how wonderful it felt to have someone who wanted to protect him.

"You've got the paperwork?"

"In my pocket."

"Good." Peony marched forwards.

The smell of his grandmother's home sent Mordecai straight back to his childhood. It filled his nostrils the moment they stepped out of the stairwell onto the landing outside her apartment. Rust and ash. Old, broken things full of old, dead memories. He tensed, and Peony took his hand.

His grandmother didn't answer the bell. He braced himself.
Grandmother?

Mordecai? What are you doing here? Her mind was heavy with suspicion.

"You don't have to be here," he told Peony in an undertone.

"I would rather be here than anywhere else."

"You should give that statement some thought. I'm sure you could think of somewhere pleasanter. A tank full of sharks, perhaps."

"Only if you were there with me."

"Thank you." She looked up at him. He attempted a smile. "For being here with me. For being you. For . . . offering to use your claws on my behalf, instead of on me."

Peony laughed. "If you would let me know who to use them

on without me having to wrench it out of your mind, I'd do it more often."

He kissed her, then straightened. *Let us in, Grandmother. It's about the Hypatia.*

The door whipped open. Aurelie Leith didn't spare a glance for the woman at her grandson's side; her eyes snapped to him, the same black, angry pits he'd long ago stopped himself from wanting to find any love in.

"The Hypatia?" Aurelie's mouth was an angry slash. "What about it? Has it burned down at last? Did Blanderley choke to death on its dust?"

13

PEONY

If she hadn't spent so much of the last day with her body wrapped around his, Peony wouldn't have noticed how tense Mordecai became the moment he saw his grandmother.

He didn't frown or jut his jaw or clench his fists. He just . . . tensed. In the actual sense of the word. Every muscle in his body turned temporarily to stone in the space between one breath and the next, which arrived perfectly on time because *of course* he wouldn't let a little thing like being scowled at by the only living member of his family make him *visibly upset.*

Staring into that fierce, suspicious face, Peony suddenly understood why Mordecai was the way he was.

Mrs. Leith's shoulders shook with rage. "Nothing good ever came of that place! It's a mistake. An ugly, money-sink of a mistake, filled with traitors! Charlatans! Tell me it's burned down, Mordecai. Give your grandmother a happy Christmas."

There it was. This was the real thing. Mordecai's revenge quest, his coldly determined plans to destroy the Hypatia—it was a pale echo of this pure *hatred* that burned bone-cracking bright in the old woman's heart.

It took Peony's breath away. Her whole chest locked tight as though her ribs were trying to protect her *own* heart against the venom pouring from Mrs. Leith's mouth.

Mordecai's mind brushed hers. She sent him a silent nod. This was what they were here for. Give his nightmare grandmother the title to the Hypatia and leave her to have a merry Christmas burning it down or something, *holy crap.*

The Hypatia. *Her* Hypatia.

Not mine, she reminded herself. *I don't even want it.*

I'm terribly sorry, Mordecai said into her mind. He stepped forward, one hand on her lower back so she couldn't help but come with him. Didn't stop her heels from skittering on the parquet floor, though.

"Um—" she began.

"Grandmother. This is Peony Fisher. She is my mate."

Wow. Such romance.

You're welcome.

Mrs. Leith's nostrils flared. Her eyes grated down Peony, once, then she sniffed and turned away, scuttling deeper into her apartment. "Your mate? I expected more from you than wasting your time on that nonsense."

"Until two days ago, I'd given the matter no thought whatsoever."

"What did she do, fall out of the sky?"

Mordecai's gaze raked across her, scalding her. "I'm the one who fell," he murmured, his voice pure silk. Peony thought a number of inappropriate thoughts, and carefully filed them for later perusal.

They followed his grandmother into the next room.

No wonder Mordecai's place is so empty, Peony thought,

wide-eyed as she took in his grandmother's living space. *If this is where he grew up.*

The apartment was dim and cramped with old, heavy furniture. Every available surface was crammed with mementoes: photo frames showing smiling people with Mordecai's eyes or jaw or nose, colored and black-and-white. There was even a wedding photo that must have been his grandmother's.

But no pictures of him. Nothing from the last thirty years.

Her heart burned with rage and hurt for him.

"Well. Congratulations to you both. I'm sure you'll be very happy together." Mrs. Leith's eyes passed through Peony briefly again as though she wasn't there, then fixed on her grandson again. "I hope you're not expecting a meal. It isn't Christmas yet. Another year gone. Another year closer to the grave, and that place is still there, mocking me. How many more years until—"

"The current owners signed over the title to me yesterday."

Grandmother went completely still. The stillness of a predator who's just sighted its prey. Except . . . not quite. "Good. Good! At last. How shall we celebrate? The 1928 Krug. Or . . . after so long . . . we could go . . . No. Not tonight. Tomorrow, maybe. Tonight . . . the champagne. Mordecai, you do the honors."

She waved Mordecai ahead of her, towards a crypt-like drinks cabinet half hidden among the other furniture. He stalked off, obediently cryptkeeper-like, leaving Peony staring.

But not at him.

Well, not *only* at him.

She doesn't want to go back to the Hypatia. Even to destroy it. All that hatred, and she's . . . afraid?

Mordecai filled three flutes with gently bubbling wine and handed one to his grandmother, then one to Peony. She accepted it with a brief glare, to remind him that he was meant to be shoving the papers at his grandmother and getting the hell out of here, not punishing himself by extending their stay. Or whatever it was he was doing.

He raised his glass. "Merry Christmas."

"Merry Christmas." Peony made sure his grandmother wasn't watching, and glared some more. His lips twitched.

Mrs. Leith snorted. "Merry Christmas indeed. How did you manage it, Mordecai? Finding your mate and taking back the Hypatia in the same week?"

"A great deal of scheming. And a great deal of blind luck." Mordecai's eyes flickered to Peony's, and she was struck by equal parts appreciation for his eyes and suspicion of them. "Peony works for the bookstore in the lower floors of the building."

"The—" Grandmother's eyes flared. "It's still there? Of course. Of course they ruined everything else and kept *that*. The bastards. Well, you're part of the family now, aren't you? Mordecai's mate." Her voice wasn't just venomous, it was death itself. And anger. Old, old anger. "Our dreams, our *vengeance*, is yours. Together, we will watch the Hypatia crumble into dust. Everything those treacherous vipers took from me. I'll snatch it out from under them. Let them see their life's work destroyed like it means nothing. I can't wait to see the looks on their faces—"

"The Hypatia isn't going to be destroyed."

What?

Mordecai's voice was calm. His mind, though—his mind kept almost brushing up against hers. It reminded her of her senior prom. The guy who'd invited her had been so nervous about being her date that he'd never *actually* touched her. Not even for photos. His hand had always hovered an excruciating inch and a half away from her. No matter that she was up for some touching. She'd been very determined about sorting the frogs from the princes as efficiently as possible back then.

But every time she'd tried to close the gap between them, he'd shimmied away like a sweaty mirage. Later, he'd admitted he was afraid that if he did, she would be so repelled that she would ditch him so fast it broke the sound barrier.

Was that why Mordecai never touched her?

Was he *afraid?*

How could he be afraid that I would leave HIM? She was a cat shifter, and he was—well, she had her suspicions what he was. He'd dropped a few hints, on purpose or not. Something big. Something that could fly. Something that had a grandmother who looked like she was half a second from breathing fire.

Whatever he was, he was strong and ferocious and rich and handsome, and she was . . .

"What do you mean, the Hypatia isn't going to be destroyed?" Mrs. Leith's acid tones seared through her distraction. "This is what we've been working towards for years! Decades of my life! Now that it's finally ours—"

"It's not ours. It's Peony's."

"What?"

For a moment, Peony was back in the bookstore during his speech. Had that only been two nights ago? But instead of staring at him from across the room as he tore her life apart, she was next to him, the backs of their hands touching.

And he was giving her everything she'd never dared ask him for.

"I intend to gift her the title as my mating gift. Land, building, and all." He held out the thick envelope to her. "It's yours. I hope you'll do something wonderful with it."

She took the envelope, feeling numb. "It's mine?"

"Yes."

"But I didn't ask you for it."

"Did you really think you needed to?" His mind touched hers. *I know you, Peony. I've seen you fly to the defense of your colleagues, your neighbors, and even me. But never yourself. That's my job. To defend you, even when you don't know you need it.*

Her chin wobbled. The Hypatia. Hers. It didn't seem real. A whole building? What was she going to do with a whole building?

"Mordecai—"

Oh shit.

Does that include defending me from your grandmother, too?

He smiled, slow and wicked and insufferably, wonderfully hers, and then turned to his grandmother.

Mrs. Leith's eyes were deep pits leading to the void at the end of the universe. "Mordecai? What is this? Some sort of joke?" She turned her death's-head stare on him. "Tell me this is a . . .

no, not a joke. Of course not. She's family, now, isn't she? She'll do the right thing. Mordecai, tell her. Make her understand."

"Nobody's going to make me understand anything!" The words snapped out of her.

So many things had changed in the last few days. She'd lost *so much*. So many dreams she'd kept squirreled away even from herself. Dreams about who her mate would be. Who *her* true self would be.

And she'd gained so much more.

"I'm not going to destroy the Hypatia. I'm going to restore it. All of it. The mezzanine over the bookstore. The weird old elevator. The lights! I've seen photos—I don't even know how they managed to hang a chandelier there, but I'm going to find out. And the rest of the building. Everything that's been ripped out or painted over or allowed to fall to pieces, I'm going to *fix*." She was vaguely aware that Mordecai hadn't exactly given her a budget for her renovations, and what she was describing might explode even the most generous budget, but that was a worry for later. Probably after his grandmother had bitten her head off. "All of it. The old apartments, the gymnasium, that ridiculous pool."

"The Riviera?" There was a strange note in his grandmother's voice.

"Everything." Peony stuck her chin out, then glanced up at Mordecai. His eyes were shining. "I want you to have a place to shift in the city and pretend you're under the stars. I want to be there with you. It'll be *our* place."

"The Riviera . . . the stained-glass stars . . ." Mrs. Leith's voice wavered.

For a moment, Peony wondered if she would break. Or bend, like her grandson had, finding something inside him that wasn't this horrific need for revenge.

"No," Mrs. Leith snarled. "It's too late for that! I'll die before I set foot in that place again! They humiliated me—it should be destroyed!"

"Let's go." Mordecai put his hand on her arm. *We've said our bit. She's said hers. It will only get worse from here. Trust me.*

"If you leave now, you'd better never come back!" Mrs. Leith's voice echoed after them.

Outside, he took a deep breath, as though he hadn't breathed the whole time they'd been inside. He tipped his head back and stared up at the night sky, thick with clouds.

Somewhere nearby, lights twinkled in a window. A Christmas carol floated on the chill night air.

"That's over," he said. "Thank God."

"Are you all right?"

He closed his eyes, a deep furrow forming between his eyebrows. "I am better than I ever have been after spending time with my grandmother," he said at last. "I wish . . ."

Peony waited.

He dropped his chin into his collar and grimaced. "I've given up wishing."

"And if you hadn't?"

He shot her a weary smile. "I wish she could find a way out. The way I have."

"Maybe she will. We can give her time. But first . . ." She

stood on her tiptoes and kissed him as snowflakes began to fill the air. "Home?"

"You already think of my apartment as home?"

"I think of anywhere I can get you naked as home." She grinned at him, and his answering smile sent a shock of joy straight into her chest. "But that apartment? I've got to be honest. Your awful apartment makes me almost understand wanting to raze a place to the ground and salt the earth behind me."

"If it's that bad . . ." He leaned in close, and this time, the touch of his mind against hers wasn't an almost-touch. It was sure and gentle and loving. *Why don't we do something about it?*

14

Mordecai

Dusk fell like a blanket over Christmas Eve. As the light faded, Mordecai woke in the ruins of his bed, more thoroughly content with his life than he had ever thought possible.

Peony stirred beside him.

"Merry Christmas, my love," he murmured.

"I want you to say it again."

"Merry—"

"The other bit."

He kissed her. "My love."

Her smile was pure feline. Satisfied and smug. He could practically hear her purring.

"How long is the drive to your parents'?" he asked.

Her eyes sprang open. She swore. "It's morning already?"

"Peony—"

"We're already late!" She jumped up.

He pulled her back into bed. "It's still evening." He kissed her, gentle and then not gentle at all. "We have time."

They had significantly less time by the time they made it out of bed.

When they finally left, darkness had not just fallen, it had pulled the covers over itself and gone to sleep. Peony put the address into his car's GPS, then explained that it would only get them three-fourths of the way there "because of all the magic or something—it's a pain in the butt". She settled into the passenger seat, relaxed and happy and glowing with a particular satisfaction that made him feel very smug.

Snow had settled all around. The city was already shaking it off, but as they left behind the brightly lit streets and tall buildings, the world outside the car quieted. Fields and hills were wrapped in white blankets, content in their winter lullaby for now—but beneath it all, a low hum of anticipation.

To his surprise, Mordecai's own heart was humming with the same anticipation. Facing the holidays without a certain level of dread was a new sensation. One he could get used to.

One he *would* get used to, with Peony at his side.

However . . . there was still one loose end to tie off.

Does she even realize it?

He could simply not mention it. Two days ago, he wouldn't have. He would have noted it, like a hole in his heart, and built up walls around it, letting it fester until the rot took hold completely. But Peony had changed him. He could be open with her.

Perhaps that's why she HASN'T mentioned it, he mused. The Peony he'd first encountered would have torn at his walls like the unholy offspring of a Valkyrie and a siege engine. But since he'd let her in, she'd softened. And—though it still galled him to admit—he needed her softness. *She doesn't want to risk hurting me by breaking down any of the walls still standing.*

It is a little bit hilarious, though, his dragon suggested.

True.

Or should I be hurt? Maybe I'm hurt. Terribly hurt. In my dignity.

Mordecai snorted gently. She caught his eye in the rearview mirror, and he tried to smile at her, only to realize he was already smiling.

"Thinking happy Christmas thoughts?" she teased.

"I'm thinking about the fact that we're visiting your family."

She sighed. "Do you want me to reassure you that it won't be as terrible as meeting your dear grandmamma? I don't think I can. My family is huge and wonderful, and you'll probably regret ever meeting me after two minutes in their welcoming presence."

"Your mother did sound excited on the phone." Peony had called her before they'd left, reassuring her family that she was on her way.

And that she was bringing someone.

"That wasn't my mother sounding excited. That was my mother repressing 99.9% of her excitement so as not to scare you off. And here you are, in the car, so I guess it worked." She flicked him a glance. "Last chance to run away screaming. Trust me, by the time they lay eyes on you, it'll be too late. You'll be in their clutches."

"I prefer being in your clutches."

Her happiness bubbled through the matebond, feather-light and shining. "I'm not planning to let you go. You'd have to take me with you as you ran away. I'm just saying, the option's there."

"I'm looking forward to meeting your family."

She gave a choked giggle. "All right. On your head be it."

"Every aspect of it appeals to me. Hordes of relatives descending on me. A labyrinth of exactly how everyone is related to you and to one another to unravel. Names to memorize. And the questions."

"The questions!" Peony's groan came directly from her soul. "Don't worry. I'll field most of them. You can stand back and look mysterious."

"An activity at which I excel," he said gravely. "I expect the majority of the questions will be for you, anyway. 'What is your shifter form?' 'Under which excruciating circumstances did you first shift?'"

Peony groaned again. "We'll have to get our story straight. I am *not* telling them what actually happened. That particular can of worms can stay shut."

"Don't worry. If all else fails, I can distract attention by shifting. It should be quite the spectacle. I haven't shifted in so long. I might need your help to think of some human thoughts to shift back."

"Promises, promises." She yawned. The reminder of how late they'd been up, and why, made his dragon let out a smug puff of smoke. "And of course, to shift into your animal form in the first place, you'll have to rustle up some appropriately . . . um . . . some thoughts typical of, er . . ."

"Yes," he said gravely.

"Um."

"We'd better get that part of the story straight as well," he deadpanned. "What sort of a shifter I am."

"You—!" Peony winced and pressed her balled fists against her forehead. "This is *not* on me. I've stolen everything else I wanted out of you from your mind or your body. I thought I'd leave you the secrecy around your inner animal out of respect." She dropped her fists and raised her chin with a sniff. "I didn't think it polite to inquire."

Her imitation of his own fastidiousness was so perfect that he laughed out loud. A smile twinkled on her face, perfect as starlight.

"Really, though." He took one hand off the wheel and twined his fingers through hers. "Have you no idea?"

"I have ideas!" she protested. "I've been thinking about it. Constantly. With only very frequent and effective distractions."

"I wondered if you could sense it the way I can your cat. Your cat makes its presence very known. I can feel it flexing its claws when it thinks I'm not looking." He sent a flicker of awareness through their connection and got an indignant bristling in return.

Peony hooted. "Oh god! It's true! I didn't know you could feel when it did that, though."

"Can you . . .?"

She opened her mouth before she'd lined up her words in the order she wanted them. He waited, enjoying the view. Her full lips with the echo of her laughter at the corners, the way she pressed them together, unselfconscious and sincere, as she harried her thoughts into place. The deep concentration as she figured something out.

You know, she looked exactly like that when—

Enough.

His dragon was right. Peony's expression was excruciatingly like the way she'd surveyed his cock the first night they were together.

He went so hard it was probably a traffic violation.

"Y-yes," she said, and the careful hesitancy in her voice was so unlike the gleeful decisiveness with which she'd approached—

No, I REALLY must stop thinking about that. Anyway, it did nothing to relieve matters.

"When I look into your eyes, I can see it. Sometimes. I think. And when I focus on the connection between us, I can sense more than you. There's another presence." She narrowed her eyes, lips still enticingly pursed. "It's new, me being able to do this. Does it only work when I look into *your* eyes? Or will I go around seeing double when I stare too hard at any shifter?"

"Or are you imagining it all and people will look at you like you're crazy if you mention it?"

She glared at him good-naturedly. "That's why I'm asking *you*. You're stuck with me, even if you do think I'm crazy."

"The feeling is mutual."

Peony snort-laughed with delight. "Oh, I'm *so* glad."

"I can see other shifters' animals when I look into their eyes. And I believe that some humans can sense it a little, as well."

"How do you know that? Oh, let me guess. You use your terrifying shifter ways to scare them into giving in at business meetings." She paused for him to respond, and when he didn't, gave a gasp of mock outrage. "You do!"

"Everyone does it. There are whole industries constructed

around teaching white-collar workers to summon their inner king of the jungle to win at office politics." He allowed himself one of his sliver-smiles and enjoyed the way Peony's cheeks heated. "I just happen to be more effective at it than others."

"But how? Your inner animal isn't terrifying. It's sweet."

What? He tried and failed to keep the surprise out of his voice. "Maybe it isn't my animal you're seeing in my eyes, after all."

His dragon echoed his shock. *Sweet? Me? No, she must have got that wrong. I'm terrifying. Roar.*

"Yes, sweet." Peony sounded defensive. "I mean, it's clearly a bit of an idiot, since it's attached to you—"

"Oh, thank you *very* much."

"You're welcome. But it's . . . curious and playful and determined. It reminds me of my cat, but less homicidal."

"I wouldn't bet on it."

"*Nothing* is more homicidal than my cat. It even wanted to murder your curtains. Poor, defenseless, boring-ass curtains."

"As I recall, it succeeded."

"Hmm . . . true. And I refuse to apologize for it."

Outside, the world flashed past. Inside, his heart was standing still. "What do you think it is?"

"It's scaly. I definitely get a sense of scaliness when I see it. And it has claws, even if it isn't as free with them as my cat." She frowned slightly and shot him a worried look. "A lizard, maybe?"

A LIZARD??!!

He laughed out loud at his dragon's dismay. "Close." *No,*

it isn't! "Scales are right, but you've got the scale wrong. Think bigger."

"A big lizard? Like an iguana? Or a Komodo dragon?"

"Partly right."

Wonder dawned on her face. "No."

"No to what?"

"You're not really— Park the car."

He pulled over as soon as there was a good place to do so. In the time it took, Peony almost started to glow with excitement. She turned and grabbed his face the moment he turned off the engine.

He submitted to her inspection. Her fingers pressed into his scalp, thumbs stroking unconsciously along the line of his cheekbones, and her eyes were a hunter's eyes.

She wasn't afraid of him. She never would be. Not his fierce, wonderful mate.

Stop hiding, he told his dragon, and it did.

"Oh," she breathed. "Hello."

Hello. Scales twitched. *Tell her I said—*

"It says hello, too."

Green fizzed through the amber-brown of her irises. Softness buffeted against his mind—and while he was reeling from the shock of *not* being affectionately clawed at, Peony's cat wriggled over to nudge against his dragon.

The intimacy floored him. This was more than physical touch, or even the delicate closeness of their minds weaving together. He'd never heard of anyone's inner animals interacting in this way.

"Oh," Peony said again. "Are . . . are they meant to do that?"

"I don't know," he admitted.

Both creatures stopped and stared at them, as though to say, *Who cares about* meant *to?*

We're going to spend the rest of our lives together, after all. Peony's voice filled his mind with petals. **I guess it's good to know they get along, too? Er. If we can count this as getting along.**

Peony's cat sharpened its claws on a convenient surface—his dragon's scales—and leapt onto its head. It yowled triumphantly and bit one of the dragon's spines.

Mordecai's dragon reared up dramatically and fell on its back, wings fluttering weakly. The cat yowled again and smacked it on the nose. His dragon was delirious with delight.

She raised her eyebrows. "Your dragon . . . *likes* how insane my cat is?"

"It does."

"Even when it tries to attack it? And you?"

"It thinks that's cute."

"Oh." Peony blinked. "It thinks my cat's inherent violence is *cute?* I think I'm offended."

"I was worried you might be."

She shot him a concerned look, and he grinned back.

"Not *that* worried, apparently," she snorted. "Fine. Being attacked by a psycho cat is *cute*."

"You have to remember, it's a dragon." He leaned across her seat, pinning her hands in a way that made her scowl and blush at the same time. "Most people who see it run away. They don't try to scratch its nose."

"It's desperate for any sort of attention, is that it?" Peony was obviously trying to look unbothered by the weight of his body pressing her into the car seat. She was failing. "So desperate it'll make do with a psycho cat. That's horrible."

"I think it's sweet." He lowered his lips to hers, stopping a quarter inch from kissing her. "I think you're cute."

"I mean it, though," she murmured, her eyes soft. "Don't get me wrong. I'm glad my cat is a fighter, not a doormat. But I don't want to be your dragon's tiny bully."

"You're not." He nestled her closer, burying his face in her hair and breathing her in. "I need someone who can stand up to me."

"By biting you?"

"If necessary." He kissed the top of her head. "I can stand a few love bites from a creature so absolutely unterrified of my dragon that it wants to chase it like a mouse."

"Oh, really?" She lifted her head and grinned at him. Light filled his heart, flowing down the magical bond between them. "Like your dragon's way of playing is rolling over on its back and pretending to be grievously wounded. Or . . . faking a sprained ankle."

Mordecai smiled. "Figured that one out, did you?" He took her hand and kissed it, fingertip by fingertip, then pressed her palm against his lips. *My dragon isn't the only one who enjoys having someone who doesn't think it's terrifying.*

Really? Because I'm sure I could manage to find you terrifying. If I tried very, very hard. Her eyes were smiling.

"I am your villain, after all," he murmured against her palm.

"The evil wizard who wanted to destroy my tower. How could I find you anything but scary?"

"Thank you," he said wryly. "I spent years perfecting my terrifying nature."

It wasn't a lie. What would he have been, if he hadn't felt he needed to present that face to the world and his grandmother?

"And I never let my dragon be anything else," he admitted. "I thought a dragon had to be fierce, and . . ." He broke off awkwardly.

Peony's gaze was understanding. "Since you had such a grand revenge planned, you and it both had to be scary enough to see it through?"

"And the other way around. Because I had this terrifying inner animal, I had to use it to further my revenge. Why would I have a dragon, if not to raze my enemies?"

They both looked inside themselves, to where their inner animals were playing in the place where their souls joined.

He was still smiling. This was ridiculous. What right did he have to be this happy?

"Every right," Peony informed him abruptly.

"I never gave it enough space to find out what it really was. Who *I* really was. My grandmother's revenge kept me from traveling . . . and there isn't any place for dragons in the city," he said.

Peony lifted her face and kissed him. "Well, I've got plans for that," she declared. "As for right now . . . Luckily, there is *plenty* of room for dragons on my family's property." Her kiss turned to a grin. "And I can't *wait* to see you transform. Thank goodness you only told me now, though. I can't imagine how crushing I would have found it when I thought my cat meant I had to be pliant and weak."

Mordecai stared pointedly at her cat, who was murdering his dragon's pointed tail. "Quite."

"You didn't know me before it," she said defensively. "Before my cat appeared, I would have died rather than be . . . be anything like I have been the last few days." She flushed hotly.

"No? No clawing?" He drew her closer. "No purchasing irritatingly inexpensive clothing when I'm trying to treat you? No romantic dates running errands for your work? No holding yourself hostage in cat form and forcing me to go to dreadful clubs?"

She grinned at him, all teeth. "I would have folded the first time you scowled at me."

"Thank god for your cat, then."

"Yes," she said and kissed him.

They untangled from one another, eventually, and then began the less enjoyable process of untangling themselves from the car.

"Ow—"

"Is that your seat belt?"

"Watch out, if I bump the handbrake, we'll roll into a ditch."

"Miss Fisher. Cars this expensive do not roll into common ditches."

She giggled. "What if you'd gotten into your car before your dragon tried to trip you up, the night we met?"

Mordecai groaned. "Don't give it ideas."

"Speaking of ideas . . ." She had that look in her eyes again. The one that made it very hard to concentrate on anything except how fast he could take her clothes off. He slid one finger beneath her collar, and she licked her lips. "This is a very quiet sort of hiding place you've parked us in. Anyone might think you had nefarious intentions, Mr. Leith."

"They would be correct."

"How terrifying." She grinned at him, smug and cat-like, and cupped him through his straining trousers. "I should remind you that we're already running late. Or . . . maybe I'm the one who lured you out here, to have my wicked way with you."

"What way would that be?"

"A way that puts you completely in my power." She worked his fly open and pulled him out, her grip intoxicatingly sure as she stroked along his length. "I promise not to bite."

He wasn't sure what noise he made, but it certainly wasn't words. Her mouth was hot and wet. She sucked him in. His thoughts dissolved. The things she was doing with her mouth, her hand, her tongue . . .

He bunched a hand in her hair. The reply that shot through their connection was instant and white-hot with desire. *Yes.*

He controlled the pace, and she controlled everything else. How hard, how deep, the hot suction of her mouth or the teasing stroke of her tongue. She kept him on the edge until white lights blinked behind his eyes. All his defenses were down.

And so were his mate's. Peony's desire enveloped him, hooked him, drew him in, and wound around him with relentless, urgent need. Her want, her wonder, her sheer joy at the noises he was making and the taste and feel of him and the fact that he was *hers* was too much.

He clenched his fist in her hair. "Peony—"

She took him in to the hilt as his hips bucked. Her heat and joy and eagerness pulled his climax from him, and she swallowed him down, leaving him breathless and floating and empty-headed.

Thoughts slowly returned. *Mine. She's mine.*

Yes. And you're mine. And now that I've got you, there's no way I'm letting you go. She nestled against him. Her kisses were light as a feather and hot as fire, and soft and sweet as the flowers she was named for.

His hands found their way under her dress and found her soaking wet. She came, shuddering, at the first explorative press of his fingers.

"Merry Christmas, my love."

They missed dinner by hours.

15

PEONY

Forget worrying about getting to her family Christmas and having to deal with all their questions about *not* finding her mate.

Now she'd found him, she got all new worries! Like getting to family Christmas at all.

And *then* dealing with their questions. All new, exciting, embarrassing questions.

Fucking half the evening away in the car had seemed like a great idea at the time. After the post-coital haze had faded (for the fifth or sixth time—she'd lost count)? Not so much.

"They're going to know," she wailed as Mordecai drove up the path to her family home. "My parents are going. To know. *Exactly* why we're late."

He shot her an entirely too smug look. "Aren't you a little old to be this embarrassed about your parents knowing you have a sex life?"

"Just . . . shh. Don't be sensible. Let me have my horrible emotions."

Wickedness flickered in his eyes. "You're sure you wouldn't prefer a distraction?"

"Behave." She let out a bone-deep sigh that started off

annoyed and ended up languid and satisfied. "For a few hours, at least. Until we can bunk off."

Mordecai chuckled. "Any last warnings before we arrive?"

"Can't remember. Sorry. If you wanted warnings, you shouldn't have screwed my brains out in the back of the car. Or the front of the car. Or . . ." She waved a lazy hand. "All the places. You remember."

"I do."

Before she could think up a rejoinder to that, they rounded the final bend before the house.

The old house sat among the trees like a comfortable old sofa. A little worn around the edges, and perhaps not exactly what you'd expect to find in the middle of a forest—at least, not in this shade of cheerful lemon yellow and sky blue—but exactly what you needed. A place to rest and enjoy good food and company . . . and maybe cause a little chaos. Swing from the rafters—why not? Slide down the roof—go for it! It was already worn around the edges. A little more fun wouldn't hurt it.

Golden light bloomed through windows lined with twinkling fairy lights. There was the dent in the front porch where her brother had missed his landing after gorging on half-fermented peaches one summer evening. The gap in the fretwork where Iris had gotten her horn stuck and refused to admit it, then stood in a noble unicorn-ish pose for hours before her mate Elaine distracted everyone into looking the other way long enough for Iris to untangle herself.

And the little corner of rooftop between the gable over

her attic bedroom and the main roof, overhung by a tree with witch-finger branches, where she'd spent so many happy hours reading and re-reading her favorite books and imagining what sort of incredibly magical inner animal she would have.

The thought didn't pang the way she thought it would. *Guess that means I'm not really upset about being a cute little cat.*

An ADORABLE little cat, said cat informed her.

With adorable sharp claws, who was willing to fight for what it wanted. And who helped her do the same.

Then the car bumped off the drive onto the big open space in front of the house where everyone else had parked, and a feeling like stepping out of the shadows into sunlight washed over her.

"Oh, it's *home*," she breathed.

"According to the directions you gave me after the GPS gave up," Mordecai said.

"I just wondered if it would feel different, now."

"Because becoming your mate meant I left my family and its skeletons behind?" He gave one of his tight smiles, and she squeezed his hand until it turned into a real one. "From all you've said, your family loves you, and you love them. I have no intention of replacing them in your heart."

"But this won't be my *only* home. You're going to buy me a house of our own, right?"

Lust and victory flared in his eyes, and his voice was a pleasurable growl. "Of course."

"The cheapest house on the block. The real estate version of no-name-brand leggings and—"

"No." He caught her chin and kissed her. "The best. Luxuries you can't even imagine."

"I can imagine a lot."

"Good. That means my gift to you will be even better." He let her go with a satisfied, wicked smile.

Peony turned her attention back to the house. "It's so late. We must have missed dinner, and the littles will be in bed. I don't know whether I should go and knock or . . ." She reached out telepathically. *Hello? Knock knock?*

Silence. And then—

Who was that?

It sounded like—

Peony??

A telepathic thrum hit that she'd never experienced before but immediately recognized: the joint excitement of her whole family, seeing her arrive home.

The front door burst open. Peony's parents were there, outlined in light. Her mom, graying-blonde hair braided into a crown wreathed with mistletoe so she would have a transparent excuse to steal kisses from Peony's dad; her dad, lanky-limbed, his dark skin shining in the light pouring past them and a telltale smudge of lipstick under one ear.

"Peony!" Her mother's voice cut through the snowy darkness. She crossed her arms. "You're late! We were expecting you hours ago!"

"I have a good excuse!" *And what an excuse. So many excuses.*

Peony's heart was full. She took a deep breath, stepped out of the car, and—

She was psychic now.

She could hear her family's telepathy. And they could hear hers.

Don't think about sex don't think about sex don't don't don't sex sex sex—

Her mother was the closest to her. She burst out laughing, hanging on to Peony's father for dear life. "Oh, sweetpea," she managed through tears of laughter. "Don't worry about it. We've all been there."

"I don't want to know that!" Peony yelped as her parents pulled her into a hug.

"Ask Elaine about when Iris—"

Do NOT ask me ANYTHING, Peony's sister-in-law demanded, her telepathic voice cutting through their parents' laughter. *At least, not in front of Iris. She's still embarrassed about it.*

Peony was tumbled from hug to hug as relatives spilled out of the house. By the time she got her balance enough to extricate herself, Mordecai was leaning against the car, a slash of darkness against the snowy backdrop.

Her heart filled her throat as she looked at him. *I love him,* she thought, then thought it again at him. *I love you.*

His crooked smile was just for her. *I heard you the first time.*

She slipped her hand into his and pulled him forward. "Mom, Dad—everyone—this is Mordecai. Mordecai—my father, Julius. And my mom, Fern."

"A pleasure."

"My sister Iris and her wife, Elaine... This is Serena, my aunt on Dad's side, and her other brothers . . . My grandparents . . ."

Peony glowed as Mordecai shook hands, introducing himself to her whole ridiculous family as they poured out the front door onto the wraparound porch.

Her family closed around them like a tide, carrying them inside. The house was decorated the same way it always was, with bright lights and streamers and every poorly hand-made ornament Peony and her siblings had ever excitedly brought home from school. Dinner was over, but the fridge was full of leftovers and no shifter in Peony's family ever said no to second dinner. They crowded around the dining table, everyone shuffling places until there was room.

"So," Peony's mom said when they were all finally sitting down. "Tell us everything."

Peony couldn't keep the laughter from her voice. "Give us a chance to eat first!"

Eat with your mouth. Dish up the story with your telepathy.

It'll be good practice, her dad added as he spooned potatoes onto Mordecai's plate. "Help yourself to the gravy there. And what can I get you from the other end of the table? Chicken or beef? It's only a light meal tonight. Tomorrow's the real deal."

Mordecai raised his eyebrows at Peony. *This is a light meal?*

Of course. Look at it. There isn't even a goose.

She didn't bother aiming her telepathy strictly at him, and from the laughter that rippled around the table, everyone heard. She didn't care. And she didn't care that they must be able to sense her feelings, as well, and the stray ripples of happiness and odd thoughts that popped into her head as she sat so close to her mate their elbows touched.

I'm so happy. So proud to have you as my mate. So glad to be here with everyone and with you.

She wanted them to know exactly how wonderful he was. How perfectly they fit. How finding him had helped her find herself.

And from the fond brushes from their minds, strangely new but utterly familiar, they understood.

He was her mate, and she'd brought him home.

The post-dinner coma found them all staggering into the living room to collapse on an assortment of sofas and beanbags. Peony fell gracelessly onto an old armchair and then grumbled as Mordecai picked her up, sat down, and arranged her on his lap.

"How are you coping?" she murmured as she nestled into him. She *did* want this to be a relatively private conversation, and even with shifter hearing, whispering was safer than accidentally fog-horning everyone's minds.

"Better than I'd expected." His eyes drooped to half-mast. "Don't ask me to recall anyone's names right now."

"I wouldn't be that mean."

"Sweetpea?" her mom called.

Peony mustered the energy to wave across the room at her. "Hey, Mom."

Fern Fisher's smile made the whole room shine brighter. "I'm glad you made it before tomorrow. It's not the same if you're not here on Christmas morning."

"The house isn't full enough for you as it is?"

Fern laughed and perched on the edge of the sofa next to Peony's chair. "Never. You know me. Not happy unless there are enough guests around to trip over."

"Oh, I'm sorry, Mom. You must be so sad right now. Only half the bedrooms full."

"Watch it, missy." Fern prodded her with her toe. "Your brother's going to head over and pick up the rest of the cousins in the morning, after they're done with stocking presents at their own houses. Little Camellia's still convinced Santa won't find them if they sleep over at a different address from the one she put on her letter to him."

"Should've emailed him."

"Mmm." Fern cast her a fond look. "But you three are the most important to have here. I could live with having no other guests at all, so long as I had my babies with me."

Unexpected tears pricked at Peony's eyes as she felt her mother's psychic touch. It was as new and as familiar as the combined energy of her whole family had been.

Fern's smile turned sad. *I know it's been hard for you. I was afraid you wouldn't come at all.*

Mom . . .

No, don't 'Mom' me. It's a hard road, having to find our mates before we find our animals. I don't know whether your brother's right and it's a blessing, or you are and it's more like a curse. Don't look at me like that. I know how much you struggled with it.

"You all found your mates so early. You built your whole lives together."

"And you didn't have anyone to show you what life could be like before you found your other half."

Peony sighed. She'd never admitted this to her mom before, but somehow it felt like she knew it already. "I felt like I was trapped in the prologue of my own life. Like I was waiting for the real story to start."

"I'm sorry, sweetpea." A troubled look passed behind her eyes, accompanied by a fluttering like heavy, feathered wings. "You don't feel like that now, though, do you? We were so proud when we heard you made manager at the store. I hope you don't think you have to leave it all behind. Your inner animal doesn't change who you are. Whatever your story is now, it's still yours."

"I know that, now. And I am going to keep the bookstore." And the rest of the building. Her thoughts soared with the possibilities.

"Good." Fern squeezed her arm. "Mates are all very well, but you need *something* to keep your mind off the bedroom."

"*Mom!*"

"I'm just saying!" She patted her on the head and laughed as Peony grumbled and shied away. *Still, it is a big adjustment. If you need space— No, not only for that, don't give me that look. I remember how hard it was to get a grip on my telepathy in the early days, that's all. If we all get too loud and obnoxious and you can't even find a quiet space in your own head, the cottage down by the boatshed is empty.*

Thanks, Mom.

Her mother's love warmed her like a palm pressed against her cheek. Peony tried to echo the action, and Fern's eyes shone.

"I love you too, sweetpea."

Peony let her gaze roam around the room as her mom went back over to sit with her dad. She'd been too busy showing off Mordecai over dinner to explore whether she really could see her family's inner animals behind their eyes while they were in human form. But now . . .

Her sister was curled up in Elaine's lap on the chaise longue by the bookshelves. Her eyes were half-shut, but Peony thought she could see a glimmer of silver in them as she curled her hands over her tiny bump. Next to them, Uncle Theo was trying to convince Elaine to join him for a game of chess. He grinned, charmingly, and she was sure the sneaky glint in his eye was his winged snake. Heath was flat on his stomach in front of the fire, playing a board game with his sons. He wasn't facing her.

Hey. She prodded him psychically, and he looked over his shoulder. There—a curious glance from something sharp-eyed and nest-proud. His griffin.

So many winged shifters, she thought absently. *I wonder if Iris ever felt left out, not having wings?* She'd always been so focused on the fact that her sister already had her inner animal, she'd never wondered what Iris's own thoughts on it were. Except for how embarrassing she found it when her horn got stuck in things.

Across the room, her dad caught her looking and raised his eyebrows. "We're all curious to see you shift, too, love. But that can wait for tomorrow. Hadn't you better take your dragon to bed?"

Peony twisted to look over her shoulder at Mordecai.

He'd fallen asleep.

His head was resting against the seat back, eyes closed, pitch lashes fluttering faintly beneath eyebrows that were only slightly less forbidding in slumber. His chest moved with slow, heavy breaths, and his arms, though they were still wrapped around her, were loose and relaxed.

It's a Christmas miracle, Peony thought, without a trace of irony. She never could have imagined the Mordecai she'd met at the bookstore letting his guard down so thoroughly in company. And yet here he was: utterly at peace. Even the deep lines at the corners of his eyes and mouth had smoothed out. He looked younger. Happier.

I barely even want to pounce on him, her cat admitted.

"Come on, Mr. Leith. Upstairs."

His eyes opened blearily as she tugged him upright. "Hmm? Oh— G'night, everyone."

Peony's childhood room was a converted attic space.

Mordecai looked around, still half-dozing, as she pulled him through the door. "Cozy," he remarked.

"Don't rub it in. I wanted the attic room so I could live my dreams of being a poor mistreated Rapunzel in the drafty tower, but Dad insisted on insulating everything and sweeping out all the spider webs."

"I can see why the Hypatia appealed so much to you."

"Ouch. Rude."

The ceiling was A-shaped, with one big dormer window looking out over the woods and the dark, starry sky. Thanks to Julius's determination that his middle child not freeze like a Gothic heroine in the winter, the room was warm and dry, even with the curtains open. She pulled them closed, and the space was even cozier: her beloved bookshelves, the lamp that sent ghostly flower patterns onto the creamy walls, the framed pictures of magical landscapes full of fairies and witches and dragons.

Mordecai ran his fingers along the frame of one of the dragon pictures, his lips twitching.

"That inaccurate, huh?"

"You'll have to wait and see." He pulled her to him for a kiss, then looked down. "That's a small bed."

"You'd better take the floor, then."

His eyes danced. "I think we'll manage."

They fell into bed together. Mordecai was asleep again within moments. Peony's thoughts were scattered; her cat was tucking itself into a tight ball inside her, tail over its nose, and Mordecai's heart beat strong and steady beneath her head.

"I love you," she whispered, and even though she was sure he'd been asleep, his arms tightened dragon-possessive around her.

Good.

She laughed and fell asleep nestled against his chest.

16

MORDECAI

Mordecai was used to waking on Christmas morning with a mixed sense of dread and sick relief. Dread because Christmas morning meant a meal with his grandmother and the anger that twisted around her like barbed wire; relief because Christmas morning meant only one day until after Christmas, when his grandmother deemed her family responsibilities over for the year and he could look forward to a precious almost-a-week on his own.

I'll never spend that time alone again. The thought filled him with a warm, heavy happiness, like his blood had turned to sweet honey.

Peony was in his arms. They were in her family home. A family where people loved each other. It felt like something from one of her books lined up against the wall: the same level of reality as a world with wizards and spells.

Which is a strange thing for someone who has a dragon in his head to think, he laughed at himself.

He'd caught snatches of Peony's conversation with her mother the night before. Fern loved her daughter with a ferocity that he would have been jealous of, except that he couldn't envy his mate anything. She deserved all the love in the world. And, having met her family, he understood why even with all that love, she'd felt out of place waiting for her inner animal to appear.

Waiting for him.

Peony frowned. "What are you thinking about? I can already tell it's bad."

"I should have found you earlier. If I'd been less focused on my revenge . . ." And, hell, how small and petty that word sounded here, surrounded by love.

She rolled on top of him and cupped his face in her hands. "If you hadn't wanted the Hypatia, you might not ever have found me. But maybe . . . maybe you would still have been happier, if you weren't paring everything out of your life that wasn't your revenge on the Hypatia board, but . . ."

He tried to imagine it. A version of himself that hadn't fashioned itself into an arrow of vengeance . . . but who'd never met Peony. "Not worth it."

The sounds of cheerful greetings and Christmas carols filtered through from the rest of the house. Peony dropped her chin onto his chest. "Three . . . two . . . one . . ."

Someone hammered on the floor from the ceiling below. "WAKE UP, SLEEPYHEAD!"

"My brother." She dragged the blankets up over her head. "He'll go after Iris next. Then he'll release his greatest weapon, the kids. We should definitely have clothes on by then."

He glanced at the bookshelves. "We could barricade the door?"

"I tried that last year. He tossed them up on the roof to come through the window."

Mordecai couldn't help the slow grin that spread across his face. "Christmas with your family is fun, isn't it?"

Amber-brown eyes found his, green sparkling in their depths. "Yeah. Come on. Race you downstairs?"

The house was alive with activity, despite the fact that it was still dark. Peony's nephews were rampaging at Iris's door, held back by Elaine, her arms firmly folded but her eyes sparkling with humor. As they passed, she knelt down and dared them in a stage whisper to see if they could jump on their dad and scare him into shifting. They scurried off, and Elaine shot Mordecai and Peony a conspiratorial glance.

"That should buy us a few minutes," Elaine called to Iris, back in the bedroom.

"But at what cost?" Iris called back.

Peony laughed and grabbed his hand. "Kitchen first. Dad's doing pancakes."

He wondered how she knew—then caught the smell of baking as they headed down the staircase. Julius was holding fort at the stove, fending off thieving hands.

And paws. And *hooves.*

Julius wielded his spatula like a sword. "Out! All of you!"

But we need our strength to go present-hunting!

Have some respect for your elders. Or pity. Whichever gets us our food first.

"Begone!"

"Since this is your first Christmas with us, I won't make you fend for yourself." Peony started forward, then paused and flexed her fingers experimentally. "Actually . . . hold my clothes?"

"Your what?"

She shifted, and her cat form flashed over to where Julius was defending the oven against his in-laws. She leapt, grabbed two pancakes in her mouth, and made it another foot across the counter before she stumbled over the trailing pancakes and went flying.

Everyone stopped. The doe with shining horns and angel wings that Mordecai guessed was Peony's grandmother, and the milky-feathered raven perched on her antlers that must be her grandfather, stared with wide eyes.

"Peony?" Julius asked. And then:

Is that our little Peony?

Come here! Let me see you!

Her cat jumped back to its feet, tail puffed up. It wavered for a moment, then picked up the pancakes again and ran.

Her grandparents raced after her. Mordecai was left alone in the kitchen with Julius, who was staring after his fleeing daughter with a stunned, happy expression.

"She's adjusting all right?" he asked.

Mordecai bundled up the clothes that had fallen to the floor when Peony shifted, then considered. "Better than I would have expected."

Julius cast him a careful look. "Better than you would have expected, given . . . ?"

"I wasn't exactly the ideal person to help her with her first shift." That was putting it lightly. "I had no idea she'd never shifted before."

"And I bet she didn't tell you, did she?" Julius chuckled and flipped a pancake onto the stack beside the stove. "No. I think you must have done just about perfect, for her to be like this today."

Someone shouted outside, "What! That's *Peony?* Peony! Come back!"

Never! A very cat-like voice shrieked with laughter in his head.

Julius's shoulders shook. "Take these through to the dining room?" he asked, pointing at the pancakes. Mordecai put the bundle of clothes under one arm and took the plate. "Oh, and Mordecai?"

"Yes?"

"Welcome to the family."

Mordecai found Peony already in the dining room, halfway up the curtains, pieces of pancakes stuck to her whiskers. She was less embarrassed than he'd expected when she finally stopped laughing enough to take back control from her cat and shift. Her grandparents retreated to their own room to do the same.

He stole a kiss as she got dressed, and she complained until he stole more. Her cheeks were pink by the time her grandparents reappeared, with more of the family hot on their heels.

Breakfast was more a series of pitched battles than a meal. Julius announced there were enough pancakes for everyone to have five each and if they wanted more they could cook them themselves, then let them at it.

Is it usually like this? Mordecai ventured to ask as Peony intercepted a bottle of syrup.

"Oh, absolutely. My family are a bunch of animals." She grabbed at a bowl of blueberry compote, but her brother got there first, carrying it away with a crow of triumph. "Actually... were you guys going easy on me before I got my cat?"

Sorry, sis, her brother admitted through a mouthful of pancakes. *Watching you with your slow human reflexes was too depressing otherwise.*

Peony snorted. *MY puny human reflexes? Who was it again who put a permanent dent in the porch because he thought he was aiming at the lawn?*

Fern caught Mordecai's eye. "Don't worry. I promise we behave ourselves better for the rest of the day. Breakfast is our chance to let our inner animals work off some energy, that's all."

Looking across the table, he could see what she meant. Everyone was back in human form now, but their animals were close to the surface, drawn out by the excitement of the holiday. The air buzzed with energy.

Interesting, he thought. Christmas at his grandmother's had been all about repressing their dragons' energies—except for their hatred.

We don't have to do that again, do we? his dragon asked tentatively.

Never.

Oh, good. It pricked its wings out. *Then should we...?*

He nodded, and his hand leapt out of its own accord—of his *dragon's* accord—and snatched a piece of bacon from Peony's plate.

She turned to him, wide-eyed. "Hey!"

He grinned and took a bite of the bacon. *I thought I'd give you the chance to show off your cat-like reflexes. My mistake.*

"Ooh, you . . . We'll see about that!"

After breakfast it was time for presents. Several carloads of further relatives appeared, and Peony's brother flew out over the woods and appeared a half-hour later with a cluster of children clinging gleefully to his back.

Grandpa Fisher gathered all the children, who ranged from toddlers to early teens, in the backyard. The sun shone bravely through a white-blue sky, catching on glittering ice and sky.

Grandpa Fisher's eyes glittered just as brightly as he informed the kids that—oh no!—Santa had been by the night before, but his reindeer had been surprised when a giant feathery creature flew up in front of the sleigh, and he'd scattered all their presents throughout the forest!

"Not again!" a little boy wailed. "Who was it this time? Was it *you*, Uncle Heath?"

"I only wanted to say hello to them!" Heath protested. The older kids hid grins. Being in on the secret was just as much fun as playing the game for real, it seemed.

"How *does* this keep happening every year?" Peony tsk'd quietly. *You'd think Santa would have figured it out by now.*

"There's only one thing for it." Heath huffed out his cheeks and put his hands on his hips. "We'll have to carry all you kids up into the trees to find your presents!"

"Hooray!"

Shifters exploded into animal form all around the yard. Mordecai watched, a strange feeling unfurling inside him, as the picture-perfect Christmas scene turned into something from a fairy tale.

He understood the benefits of an exercise like this: none of the children were shifters, so they couldn't communicate with the adults telepathically when the adults were in animal form. This forced them to find other ways to communicate: sign language, body language. There was no guarantee the children would find their mates early. Being able to understand their shifter relatives without the use of telepathy would be a vital skill as they grew up. The grown-ups had to slow down to make sure the kids understood and were safe, and the kids got to order them around and see their parents and aunts and uncles make fools of themselves scrambling after brightly-wrapped presents. The older children got to explore the bridging gap between childhood and adulthood, taking on some of the responsibility of knowing it was all a game while honing their own skills and looking out for the littler ones.

It was a good ploy, all said.

But that wasn't why he felt so strange.

"Auntie Iris, will you help Jessamine and me?" A tweenager approached them, holding the hand of an awed-looking child of some other, younger age. Mordecai hunted through his brain for references to child ages and came up blank.

Younger than twenty, his dragon suggested.

He snorted. *Yes. Technically correct. I am fairly sure the tiny tot who barely comes up to my knees is younger than twenty.*

"Of course! Elaine and I would love to help you find your presents." Iris transformed into an ethereal unicorn. Beside her, Elaine shrugged herself into a massive bear. The two kids jumped on their backs, and they headed off into the trees.

"What if the presents are high up in the trees?" Peony called after her sister.

Then Elaine will throw the kids up! Iris shouted back.

Peony did an exaggerated double-take. "You'll *throw* them into the trees?"

Jessamine shrieked with delight.

Peony shook her head. "At least with the flying shifters, you don't need to worry about someone catching you on the way down."

"But I don't want to fly *or* be thrown," said a small voice.

Mordecai looked down. A little boy was staring up at the trees with a worried expression. He couldn't have been much older than five or six. Probably. "What's your name?"

"Briar." His eyes widened. "Are you Peony's husband? Who's a dragon?"

New traveled fast in his mate's family. From the amused noise Peony made, his cheeks had just gone an interesting color. "We're not married." Yet.

Yes, YET, Peony agreed placidly. *One of us has to ask the other, first. You'd better be quick about it if you want to get in first.*

"But I am the dragon shifter."

Briar looked around. Mordecai and Peony were among the last adults left in front of the house, and the others were all flying shifters. He looked at Peony. "And you're a cat?"

"That's right." She shot Mordecai a self-deprecating thought. *Days of drama over what my inner animal is and what it means about my soul, but to most of the people here, I'm just Auntie Somebody.*

"Cats are small."

It wasn't hard to follow the poor kid's train of thought. If scared old Santa had been careless enough to drop his presents up high, his choices were either cling to someone's back and fly up into the canopy—something he clearly didn't want to do—or wander around on the forest floor and hope someone shook them down.

Being thrown around by Elaine probably didn't appeal, either.

Peony kneeled down in front of Briar, a mischievous grin on her face. "That's right. My cat is *very* small. But you know what it's good at?" She looked up at Mordecai. "Climbing."

Mordecai hadn't been exaggerating when he'd said he didn't shift in the city because there wasn't room. No one could miss a creature the size of his dragon flying around the skyscrapers.

But out here? He was the perfect size.

Don't ruin your clothes, Peony warned him. *Not all of us can afford to replace our mate's wardrobe when they run mad and transform without planning to.*

Mordecai narrowed his eyes at her mock-seriously and ducked behind the corner of the house to undress. He called on his dragon as he tucked his socks into his shoes and set them tidily against the wall.

Really? Here? Now?

We've been asked to help, he said, and the strange feeling inside him suddenly made sense. He'd been looking at the Fishers' present-hunting tradition as though he was an outsider. But he wasn't.

This is Peony's home. But it's mine now, too. And these are my people.

Hurry up? Please? Peony's voice brushed against her mind. **I know I've been playing it super cool, but I REALLY want to see your dragon form.**

He acquiesced.

Snow sheeted away from him in great drifts as his dragon took form. He unfurled his wings and gloried in the brisk chill of winter air on their leathery skin, the skitter of ice sliding over his scales. He shook himself and caused a minor snowstorm.

His dragon was sinuous and long, with nimble-clawed legs and a forked tail that slithered on the garden tiles like it had a mind of its own. *No wonder Peony's cat kept chasing it,* he thought. His scales gleamed moodily. They were black except for an ember-like glow at the root, almost invisible where each scale overlapped with its neighbor. Standing in front of the candy-colored Fisher house, he must have looked like a leftover from Halloween.

But none of that mattered, because Peony was gazing up at him with stars in her eyes.

Our mate likes how I look? his dragon asked.

Yes. His huge, scaly, needle-clawed, black dragon. He'd always thought it looked like the sort of creature a hero would slay, and that made it easier to build himself up as the villain. But Peony was looking at him like he was a knight in shining scales.

"Wherever we end up living, it has to be somewhere you can safely shift," she breathed. "And where you can take me flying."

"I don't *want* to fly," Briar protested.

"That's okay. We're not going to fly on Mordecai. We're going to use him as a ladder." She grinned at the small boy. "Watch me after I shift. I'm going to jump onto his leg and climb aaaaall the way up onto his back and then aaaaall the way up to his head, where I'm going to look around for presents. Do you want to come with me?"

"Yeah!"

Mordecai's dragon held still as Peony and her little cousin picked their way up its back. Peony tapped her paw where Briar could find a good handhold, and Mordecai kept his wings stretched out to form a safety net if Briar lost his balance. But the little boy was as sure-footed as he was sure he didn't want to go flying. When he reached Mordecai's head, he sat firmly behind his horns, buzzing with excitement.

Ready to go? Peony asked, chirruping the same question to Briar. She laughed silently. *He's nodding. This communication problem thing goes both ways, huh?*

With Briar as navigator, Peony as translator, and Mordecai providing the essential service of being a very long dragon who could raise his head giraffe-like to the very tops of the trees, they headed into the woods. Snow sheeted off his wings and sides as he wound through the trees. Above, the sky was full of strange and wonderful creatures. Griffins flew wing-to-wing with winged horses, huge eagles, and chimeric animals he didn't even have a name for. Below, Iris picked her way delicately through the wintry undergrowth. The older kid with them walked ahead of her, pulling low-hanging branches out of the way of her horn, and Jessamine howled with laughter as Elaine tossed her a few feet in the air with every step.

Mordecai rehearsed what names he could remember as they wandered deeper into the woods, checking with Peony when he couldn't match a name to a face (furry or otherwise). The silvery winged snake was Peony's Uncle Theo; the delighted child throwing him into the branches to wind around a present was her cousin Astaria.

Or my second cousin? Third? I can never remember how these things work.

I'm still trying to decide whether the floral naming scheme is helpful or not.

It used to be, when it was all of us from Mom's side. But then the others started naming their kids after plants too, the cheats, and now it's a free-for-all. Ooh! Look! She nudged Briar with one soft paw. *I see your name on that present!*

The gift was dangling from a high branch a few trees away. Mordecai balanced himself carefully as Briar stretched forwards, using the dragon's horns as safety handles that no OSHA office in the world would have considered compliant. "Look! That one's for me!"

The boy's excitement was so vivid, it was hard to believe he wasn't already telepathic. Mordecai laughed silently—and his dragon made a soft chirrup-chuffing noise that was *its* laughter.

You've never done that before, he told it, amazed.

I've never had so much fun before! Look! Tell Peony there's another present for Briar up ahead!

It didn't sound resentful of the years they'd spent *not* having fun. Or the ways Mordecai had tried to make it something it wasn't.

Of course I don't. It sounded puzzled. *If I didn't know what I was meant to be, how could you? We were figuring it out together.* It sighed happily. *And then our mate figured it out for us.*

17

Peony

"I'm beginning to worry about my cat," Peony admitted, nestling closer against Mordecai's side.

They were snuggled into the same oversized armchair as the night before, this time for a post-lunch nap rather than a post-dinner one. Technically, they were supervising a gaggle of her younger cousins playing in front of the Christmas tree; really, they were doing about as good a job as Uncle Theo, who was wrapped around the Christmas tree in snake form and was beginning to snore.

"Your cat?" Mordecai's concern flicked over her, the psychic equivalent of touching someone all over to see if they were hurt.

She wriggled happily. "I haven't heard so much as a peep out of it since lunch."

Not true, it said lazily. *Peep. Zzzz.*

"You've worn it out," Mordecai suggested.

"Impossible." She stifled a yawn. "It's not even mid-afternoon yet. There are so many decorations it hasn't pounced on yet. So many—*ahhhh*—bits of tinsel it hasn't mauled."

"Give it time."

"Mmm." She ran her toes up his leg. His hand tightened around her waist. Maybe going to the boat-shed cottage later *was* a good idea. "Sorry I didn't get you any presents."

He laughed softly. "Is this where I tell you the only present I need is you?"

I didn't even wrap myself nicely for you! She fake-groaned and let her head fall back against his chest. **Worst mate ever.**

I beg to disagree. And I haven't bought you anything, either.

Um. You bought me an entire BUILDING.

That was yesterday.

Oh, well, fine. Have fun outdoing that for my actual gift. It was a good thing he was behind her and couldn't see her grinning like the Cheshire Cat as she grumbled away inside her head. Then again, he had a direct line to her heart; he didn't need to see her smile to know she was drunk on happiness. **I don't know how I'm going to compete.**

Take a leaf out of your cat's book and fall asleep, Mordecai suggested. **Like your uncle over there. I didn't know snakes could snore.**

"Bet you didn't know they could have wings, either." Speaking out loud had been a mistake—she yawned again, and her eyelids drooped. "You think you're up to watching the kids by yourself?"

They seem relatively harmless, he said confidently.

She snorted. "You say that now. Wait until they realize two of their jailers are asleep and the one that's left is trapped under a sleeping dead weight." She'd been an adorable tiny child playing sweetly on the rug herself, once upon a time. She knew how it worked.

"You forget." Mordecai's breath tickled her ear tantalizingly.

"I'm the terrifying dragon shifter who holds whole companies in my thrall. I can manage a few children."

"Famous last words."

One moment. Mordecai sat upright, holding her so she didn't slide to the floor as he turned, frowning, to look in the direction of . . . the far wall?

"What are you—"

He swore and leapt to his feet, holding her tight. Tension ratcheted through his body, and a surge of dread flowed to her down the matebond. She reached for him psychically and stopped.

His shields were up again.

Mordecai? She reached out again, one careful tendril of love.

He looked at her, ruefulness battling with stress in his eyes. "I'm sorry for whatever's going to happen now," he said in an undertone. "Tell your family I'm going to take care of it."

"Of what?"

A gleeful shout from outside interrupted them. "Another dragon!"

Mordecai's grandmother landed on the forecourt. Her dragon form was as elegantly sinuous as his, but her scales were a deeper blood-red, and her horns curled back from her head like a ram's.

Her voice thundered into Peony's mind. It tasted of ash and rust, the same scent that had pervaded her home. *Here you are. Good. I hoped to find you before you got too far.*

She's speaking as though he's running away, Peony thought, and outrage sizzled in her veins. As though now that Mordecai had given up on her toxic plans for him, he would scurry away like a mouse, not the noble dragon that he was.

"Grandmother." Mordecai's voice was calm. If Peony hadn't been holding his hand as they stood together on the porch, she wouldn't have had any idea of the tremor of tension running through his frame. "Merry Christmas."

Disbelief and the taste of ash mixed with rain rolled through Peony's mind. Around them, the members of her family who'd heard the news of another dragon winced.

Her mom sent her a worried glance. *Is everything okay?*

This is Mordecai's grandma.

Oh! That's . . . lovely?

More like complicated. But we're handling it.

Mordecai took a deep breath. His shields were lowered again, and her heart ached at the turmoil she sensed in him. It was a show of how much he trusted her that he let her see it. On the outside, he was cold and controlled.

Inside, he was holding on to the threads of a happiness he had only known for a few hours and was desperate not to lose. She touched his thoughts, and her breath caught in her throat.

If Peony's family knows where I come from, really, would they still welcome me as one of their own?

Of course we would, she told him roughly. Her cat was wide awake now, hissing with rage. How dare his grandmother come here and make him so vulnerable?

"I thought you said you never wanted to see us again!" Peony shouted, letting go of Mordecai's hand and striding in front of him. "Funny way you've got of showing it."

Aurelie turned her lizard-like head towards her. Thin streams of smoke whispered from her nostrils. *So I did.*

Aurelie's dragon eyes were the same as her human ones: hard and hateful, as though everything she saw was an enemy.

Peony held her gaze. *Mordecai took the worst of your awfulness last time,* she thought grimly. *I'm not going to let him do the same now.*

"Why are you here?" she demanded. "You made it clear yesterday that you didn't have any use for Mordecai if he wasn't going to stick with your horrible crusade. Your revenge is over. The Hypatia is *mine*. Mordecai gave it to *me*. And I'm not going to abandon it or destroy it to make you feel better about losing it. I'm going to rebuild it. The arcade. The apartments. Even the *pool*," she decided in a rush of confidence, with an apologetic aside to Mordecai about how much it was likely to cost.

The cost doesn't matter. He sounded dazed.

"By the time I'm done with it, the Hypatia isn't just going to be the way it used to be. It's going to be *better*. The board are going to be sick every time they see it, and they're not going to be able to avoid it, because it will be *brilliant*. Like a star stolen straight out of the sky for everyone to enjoy."

For a moment, she wasn't sure if the old dragon was going to burn her down or leap forward and devour her in a single bite. Then a tremor went through her. Her wings, the color of cooling embers, sagged.

Thank you, she said, her voice a rusty croak. *For saving

Mordecai from me, and for showing me that I was wrong. I thought I wanted to destroy the Hypatia. But to have it restored to all its glory, not a ruin that reminds me of my shame every time I see it . . . that would be better. I didn't see that until now.*

She collapsed in on herself. One of Peony's aunts ran forward with a dressing gown in her arms and wrapped it around the old woman as she shifted back into human form.

Aurelie's sharp eyes found Peony's again. She nodded once, exhausted, then gathered her dignity back around herself as though she was wearing a fur coat, not a fluffy pink robe. "As for you, grandson of mine—" Mordecai tensed, and Aurelie relented. "I'm sorry. That's why I came here. To thank your little spitfire mate for taking you away from me, and to apologize to you. You deserved a better grandmother than I have been to you. I should never have made my anger your problem to deal with."

Mordecai hesitated before he answered. "Thank you for saying that," he said at last. "And for coming out here."

"I couldn't leave things the way we did yesterday." Aurelie twisted her neck, and Peony saw the echo of her dragon shuffling its wings in the movement. "But I've said my bit, now. I'll wish you merry Christmas and leave you to your mate's good care."

Mordecai's emotions were in turmoil. Peony put her arm around him, and he sent an image into her mind: his grandmother's apartment. Not the way he saw it, but the way she had. The cold. The dust. The rows of photo frames full of the people she'd lost, and the emptiness everywhere else in her home.

She's right, he said. *You saved me. If I hadn't met you, I would have ended up the same way she did. Just as lonely and miserable. She was all I had, and I didn't know how else to be until I met you. But I don't think she did, either.*

She still hurt you, she reminded him gently.

I know. I'm not going to pretend I'll forget and forgive. But this can be a start, at least. He put his arm around her, his eyes warm. The broken glass in them wasn't sharp and jagged-edged anymore; it was melting into something brighter. Like the night sky in a blazing, faceted jewel, catching the light and reflecting it back in shimmering joy. *Why destroy when we can start to rebuild?*

She nodded, a silent approval of what he was about to propose.

Mordecai raised his head and held out one hand to his grandmother. "Stay for dinner?"

That night, they went to the little cottage on the lake. Someone had fallen through the ice earlier—Peony suspected her brother—but the hole was already freezing over.

It was the perfect Christmas scene. Snowy and calm, with hints of hidden chaos.

"How are you feeling?" she asked Mordecai as they made their way up the path to the cottage.

"About my grandmother?"

"Don't feel like you have to limit yourself. About anything. Everything." She tugged his chin down until she could kiss him.

I'm not hiding anything from you any more, he reminded her. *All my walls are down. You can find out for yourself.*

"Ah, but I'm selfish and incorrigible and want to hear you say it."

"Very well. Since you asked so kindly. I'm happier than I ever thought I would have the right to be." His expression was clear as he tipped his head back to stare at the stars, hands in his pockets. "I've spent my life looking towards the future. This is the first time I've looked forward to it, instead. Because of you."

"It's going to cost you a lot." She slipped her hand into his pocket and held his tight.

"Bringing back the Hypatia? A building so decrepit even the rats have fled?"

"It has rats! Er. That came out wrong." She cleared her throat. "It has the normal number of vermin, a fact about which I am not weirdly defensive," she said as seriously as she could manage.

Mordecai laughed aloud. "Five fewer vermin, now the board don't have their claws in it." He wrapped his hand around hers. "Like I said, I'm looking forward to it. What's the use of having money if I can't use it well? And now I'm not focused on my grandmother's revenge . . ." He shook his head. "I still can't believe she came out here. I can't believe she *apologized*."

Aurelie had stayed for dinner. Faced with Peony's horde of relatives, she'd let her haughty mask crack—and beneath it had been a tired, unsure old woman, who'd been unhappy too many years to remember how to be anything else. Peony's chest tightened at the thought of Mordecai becoming like that.

"I'm glad she did," she said out loud, and Mordecai nudged her in a way that told her he'd heard her thoughts. "I'm also glad she agrees I'm the best thing to ever happen to you."

"I can only hope you'll say the same about me one day."

She rounded on him and searched his eyes for a glint of humor, but he was being completely sincere. "What? Mordecai, you *are*. How can you think that you're not?"

He gestured stiffly. "I've given you the Hypatia. Financial security." She snorted. "Monetary things. You joke about not being able to match my Christmas gifts, but it's the other way around. You've given me a new way of being myself. You've rescued my soul, Peony. Nothing I've done can equal that."

"You really still think that?" She stood in front of him and took his face in her hands. For a moment, they were back in the office at the bookstore, on the verge of the kiss that had changed her life forever. "You've saved me as much as I saved you. You've helped me figure out who I am—not just my cat. I'm not only talking about the magic." She gazed into his eyes. "I used to think my life was a prologue. You've made me see that I was never just waiting around for my life to start. I was already living it. And now I get to start the best chapter of all."

He stared down at her. She felt the moment he accepted what she was saying as the truth. It wasn't a wall inside him, falling down; it was his heart opening. *My mate. Joining you in your story would be the greatest adventure of my life.*

I'm glad you don't need any more convincing. A smile tugged at the corners of her lips. *But just in case you do . . .*

She kissed him, and it was even more magical than the first time.

A NOTE FROM ZOE CHANT

Thank you for reading *Her Purr-fect Mate*! I hope you enjoyed reading it as much as I enjoyed writing it. Christmas is a perfect time for romance; add a little magic and what's not to love?

If you would like to find more of my books, join my newsletter, or discover my VIP Readers Facebook group, please visit my website: www.zoechant.com

ALSO BY ZOE CHANT

Have you read all of my Christmas shifter romances?

A MATE FOR CHRISTMAS

A Mate for the Christmas Dragon
Christmas Hellhound
Christmas Pegasus
The Hellhound's Un-Christmas Miracle
Christmas Griffin

CHRISTMAS VALLEY SHIFTERS

The Christmas Dragon's Mate
The Christmas Dragon's Heart
The Christmas Dragon's Love

SHIFTERS FOR CHRISTMAS

A Griffin for Christmas
A Dragon for Christmas
A Hippogriff for Christmas
A Unicorn for Christmas
A Hellhound for Christmas

www.ingramcontent.com/pod-product-compliance
Ingram Content Group UK Ltd.
Pitfield, Milton Keynes, MK11 3LW, UK
UKHW041449180426
11946UKWH00002B/20